"You tried to kill him tonight, didn't you?"
Angel went on. "And you shot me."

He had appeared on the railing of the loft—jumping up, in order not to be heard climbing the creaky wooden stairs. Slade whirled, pointing his gun at Angel, who was in full vampire mode.

"I'll do it again, too, demon," Slade said.

"I'm already dead."

Slade turned the gun away from Angel—and pointed it at Cordelia again. "Maybe you are dead," he said. "But *she's* not."

Cordelia looked down the barrel of the big gun. It was as black as the inside of a grave, and seemed as wide and deep. "Um, Angel? I think maybe he means it."

"I'm sure he does," Angel hissed. He leaped.

Slade fired.

Angel™

Available from POCKET PULSE

The Essential Angel Posterbook

Available from POCKET BOOKS

ANGEL™

hollywood noir

Jeff Mariotte

An original novel based on the television series
created by Joss Whedon & David Greenwalt

POCKET PULSE

New York   London   Toronto   Sydney   Singapore

Historian's Note: This story takes place during the first half of *Angel's* first season.

An *Original* Publication of POCKET BOOKS

 POCKET PULSE published by
Pocket Books, a division of Simon & Schuster, Inc.
1230 Avenue of the Americas, New York, NY 10020

ISBN: 0-7434-0697-4

First Pocket Books printing January 2001

10 9 8 7 6 5 4 3 2 1

POCKET PULSE and colophon are registered trademarks of
Simon & Schuster, Inc.

Printed in the U.S.A.

For the people who sell mysteries day in and day out: Terry, Patrick, Elizabeth, Linda, and Beth at Mysterious Galaxy, and legions of others at specialty stores across the country

Acknowledgments

This book owes a huge debt to those writers who invented hard-boiled fiction and made it worth reading: Dashiell Hammett, Raymond Chandler, and especially Ross Macdonald. One more name belongs here, because of the particular era to which this book makes reference—George Clayton Johnson, who wrote *Ocean's Eleven*, the first and probably best of the Rat Pack movies from 1960. Many, many writers have built on what they did, and to name some would be to leave others out, so I won't even try.

It also, in a more immediate way, owes much to the people who helped me, cheered me on, encouraged me, or badgered me to work—Lisa Clancy, Micol Ostow, and Liz Shiflett for Pocket, Caroline Kallas and Debbie Olshan for Fox, Chris Golden, Scott Ciencin, and Greg Rucka for inspiration.

Also huge thanks to Nancy and Maryelizabeth, and Holly, Belle, and David.

PROLOGUE

The building was on Argyle Avenue, south of Hollywood Boulevard, on a corner almost dead center between Hollywood and Sunset. It had stood there since its construction in 1921. It had been, at various times, a hotel, a tailor shop with apartments above it, an office building, and a haven for homeless squatters and runaways. For the last four years it had been abandoned completely, its windows boarded over with sheets of plywood tagged with graffiti, its doors nailed shut, door-knobs stolen. Most locals didn't look twice at it. Kids occasionally told one another it was haunted, as kids tend to do with vacant buildings. No one really believed that.

Now it was coming down.

A tall chain-link fence surrounded it, blocking the sidewalk. Tied to the fence were signs: Sidewalk

Closed, Use Other Side and Hard Hats, Work Boots, Long Pants Required. Also No Radios. No Dogs.

Jackhammers thundered inside the building, tearing it apart brick by brick, wall by wall. Workers punched out walls with sledgehammers. Dust billowed from the gaping windows. The building was too close to the street and neighboring structures to be dynamited, and it was hardly big enough to warrant it, just six stories. A narrow alley ran behind it, with a couple of parking places for people who had worked in the building. The parking places were filled with glass and trash now. In a matter of days, the refuse would be carted to the dump and a corner strip mall would be built in its place: a convenience store, a dry cleaner, a take-out pizzeria.

Urban renewal, Hollywood style.

"Listen," Barry Fetzer demanded. "I need to get in there."

Randy Blake chewed on a wooden toothpick and squinted through the chain link at Fetzer. His goggles were parked on his forehead, and dust from the demolition settled around them as they spoke. Randy wore a plaid flannel shirt over a stained gray T-shirt, paint-spattered jeans, work boots, and a hard hat. Barry Fetzer wore a suit that probably cost as much as Randy made in a week, and Randy was not only a union member, but a foreman as well.

"I don't think so," Randy said, shouting to be heard over the din.

"I don't think you understand. I'm—"

"I don't care if you're the governor, you don't come onto this job site without a hard hat and work boots. You got a hard hat?"

"You could lend me yours."

Randy took his off, looked at the back of it where he'd carefully printed "Blake" in big black letters.

"Is your name Blake?" he asked.

"No, I told you, my name is Fetzer. Barry Fetzer."

Randy put his hat back on. "Then I don't think you can wear my hat."

"Listen," Barry pleaded, running his fingers through his silver-flecked hair. "Why are you giving me such a hard time, Mr. Blake?"

Randy chewed on the toothpick for a while, thinking that question over.

"Could be it's because I got a building comin' down around us here," he finally answered. "And you show up with no paperwork, no I.D. except your driver's license, and give me a story about how you're here on behalf of the head of the Department of Water and Power and you have to get into this building. Well, A, there ain't no water in this building, and B, it's dangerous in there and you, speakin' quite frankly, Mr. Seltzer, don't strike me as a man who's used to dangerous situations."

"I'm not asking you to be responsible for me," Barry responded indignantly. "And the name is Fetzer."

"This's my job site," Randy told him. "I'm the foreman. That makes everyone here my responsibility. And unless you got a warrant or some other legal authority, you're not gettin' into this building. Wait a couple of days and go down to the city dump, and you can pick through the rubble, if there's something you're lookin' for."

Fetzer flapped his arms in aggravation. Randy watched him with some amusement, thinking the guy might actually stamp his foot next. One could always hope.

"What's your name again?" Fetzer asked after some consideration.

Randy turned his head, letting Fetzer read the back of his hard hat once more. When he turned back, Fetzer had taken a little notebook from one of the pockets of his Italian silk suit and was carefully writing something down. Finished, he clicked his pen angrily, closed the notebook, and tucked it away. "Well, Mr. Blake, you can be sure your employers will be hearing about this."

"Hope so," Randy said. "I could use a raise."

Fetzer turned on his Bruno Maglis, gave the blue plastic wall of the site's PortaJohn an angry punch, and stormed away. Randy watched him disappear toward Sunset, then went back into the building.

After a moment, Jimmy Socolich came to him,

something like panic in his eyes. "Boss!" Jimmy called. Jimmy addressed almost everyone as "boss," so it wasn't necessarily a sign of respect.

"What's up, Jimmy?"

"You gotta see this, boss. Right now, I think." Jimmy's voice was tinged with something—excitement or maybe fear. He hadn't been in the country that long, and sometimes his accent was a little on the thick side.

"What? What is it?"

"Just come, boss. You see."

Randy lowered his goggles over his eyes and followed Jimmy Socolich's compact, wiry form up the stairs to the fourth floor. Jimmy passed through a remarkably well preserved wooden door with a pane of glass inset into it, remarkably unbroken. Inside a space that had been some kind of office, three workers were standing around a wall. Randy pressed his way into the room. "What's going on?" he asked.

"Look here, Randy," Crystal Stiles said. She pointed inside a closet in an interior office. "There's a brick wall there," she said.

"Yeah?" Randy asked. There were lots of brick walls hereabouts. Brick wasn't the most common of building materials in Los Angeles, but it wasn't unheard of.

"It's in the wrong place," Crystal said. "Look, it's about eighteen inches away from the real wall."

Randy looked at where she was pointing. She was right. The wall the closet backed up against was a foot and a half behind this inside wall. This brick wall, which seemed to postdate the original building construction, jutted out from the real wall by at least eighteen inches. That could mean there was a hidey-hole behind this wall.

"And look at the masonry," she continued. "It's awful."

Randy examined the mortarwork. Sloppy, amateurish. If the wall hadn't been inside a closet, and only a few feet wide, it probably wouldn't have lasted very long.

"Well, what are you waiting for?" he asked. "Get into it."

"Yes, sir," Crystal responded with enthusiasm. She raised her sledge, eyed her target, and brought it home. A chunk of the wall turned to powder.

"Good shot," Randy said, touching her shoulder. "Now let's get a light in there. Who's got a light?"

Jimmy Socolich put a flashlight in Randy's hand, and he stuck it through the hole Crystal had made, playing it around the black space behind the wall. Definitely added after the building was constructed, Randy decided.

Then the light fell on something. He stopped it. Studied it.

He felt sick. He handed the light to someone behind him. "Take a look," he said.

Crystal snagged the flashlight, shone it through the hole. But Randy couldn't look away. He squeezed in next to Crystal, peering through the hole with her.

Inside was a corpse, decades old. Insects had picked the skull clean except for a couple of patches of scalp that remained, with random strands of hair attached. Remnants of a suit still clung to the desiccated body. When the light played across the hollow eye sockets and the grinning teeth, the thing seemed to move, almost to come alive.

Randy felt Crystal shiver.

Then he felt something else, a cool, fetid breeze from inside the wall, blowing across—no, *through* him. This time, Crystal's shivering was nearly uncontrollable, and Randy was shivering too.

It was as if something unclean had passed through his body. It felt like he imagined a thousand cockroaches covering every inch of his body would feel. His skin crawled.

Behind him, Jimmy Socolich shuddered, then dropped to his knees in prayer.

The other workers looked away from each other, suddenly uneasy in one another's company.

"Randy—" Crystal started.

"Yeah?" he asked.

"Nothing."

He looked at his boots. "Don't touch anything," he said, his gaze fixed on their scuffed leather surface. "I'll call the police."

"Yeah, you do that," Crystal said.

When Randy went downstairs to find his cell phone, Jimmy Socolich was still on his knees.

CHAPTER ONE

Angel was restless.

He sat behind his desk in his inner office, staring into space. In the front office, Cordelia and Doyle were talking, laughing, moving about. Cordy was a stunning former cheerleader who had moved to Los Angeles from Sunnydale and created a position for herself in Angel's business. Doyle, half demon and half human, conveyed messages from the Powers That Be. They were both invaluable aides to Angel. But at that moment they were only at the periphery of his awareness, and he wasn't part of their conversation.

He thought about getting up, going out to the front office, sitting down on the couch, and taking part. He also thought about going outside to see if anything was going on in the city that he ought to be aware of. Each thing he thought of doing superseded the one he'd thought of before, and he ended up doing nothing.

What's the matter with me? he wondered

He stayed in his seat, gaze fixed on nothing in particular.

"What's Angel's problem?" Cordelia Chase asked. She twirled her long brown hair around two fingers as she spoke. "I poked my head in there a couple of minutes ago to listen for his breathing, just to see if he was still—well, not alive, but you know what I mean. But then I remembered, there's no breathing either. Finally he blinked, though, so I guess there's no need for vampire CPR or anything."

"I reckon he's bored," Doyle said, running a hand through his black hair. "We were talkin' last night, and he said he thought it was comin' on again. Said he gets in these moods."

"Angel said that?"

"Well, you know, I had to read between the lines a bit."

"Well, we all get moods, but some of us can, you know, go shopping, or take Pamprin or something. Hasn't he ever heard of getting over it?"

"You've known him longer than I have, Cordy," Doyle replied. "But you gotta figure he's been around for, what, almost two hundred and fifty years now. Talk about 'been there, done that.' If there's anything he hasn't done, especially in the first hundred years or so of his misspent youth, I don't want to know about it. He said sometimes it just sneaks up on him, this feelin' of havin' done it all and seen everything."

Cordelia stood up from her desk and walked over to the couch where Doyle sprawled. His shirt was bright blue, making his piercing blue eyes seem to sparkle even more than usual. He wore a dark leather jacket, unbuttoned, and dark pants. He wasn't a bad-looking guy, and except for the fact that he never seemed to have any money, she might have let him ask her out sometime.

"Sounds like you two had quite the male-bonding session." There was more than a trace of sarcasm in her tone.

"Oh, we bonded all right," Doyle replied in his distinctive Irish brogue. "There was serious conversation, there were manly punches to the arms, there was even the consumption of liquids. Pig's blood, in his case, but still . . . There was everything except testosterone-fueled hugs at the end of it."

Cordelia rolled her eyes. "Must have been quite the spectacle. Was this in a public place? I guess not, with the blood-drinking and all."

"The blood was only for him, I wanna remind you. My beverage came from a bottle, not a butcher."

"Right." She sat down next to him and continued in a hushed voice. "So with all this bonding and beverages, why is he still bored? I hate to say it, considering I wasn't invited along, but it sounds as if you had a fun evening."

"One night of carousin' with your chums—or chum, as the case may be—don't necessarily overcome a coupla hundred years of same-ol'. He said when we started the detective agency—"

"You mean the one I pressured him to start," Cordelia said proudly.

"The very one. Anyhow, he said that he thought it'd keep him interested. You know, each new person through the door'd be a new and different kind of case. He'd see the whole range of human existence, right here in his own foyer."

"Is that what this is, a foyer?"

"I'm paraphrasin', all right?" Doyle snapped. "But instead, his last three cases have been, what?"

Cordelia thought about it for a moment. "Let's see," she said quietly. "That runaway cat, Mr. Stripey. The guy with the hardware store who thought he was being overcharged by his suppliers—paperwork, big yawn. Oh, and then Mr. Stripey ran away again." She glanced through the office window at Angel, still sitting in the same position, a glazed look in his eyes. "Okay, point taken. And maybe we should send Mrs. Finnegan a fake change-of-address notice, so next time Mr. Stripey runs away she won't be able to find us."

"That's what I like about you, Cord," Doyle chuckled. "Your utter lack of a conscience."

"I have a conscience," she protested, sounding somewhat hurt. "Well, when I want to. Anyway, I think they're overrated, unless there are talking crickets involved. I mean, look at Angel. Think he'd just be sitting there in his office letting moss grow on him if he didn't have a conscience? No, the old Angelus would be out biting, killing, maiming, having a great old time."

"Right," Doyle agreed brightly. "And he'd start with those closest to him—like us."

"Another good point. Maybe he's better off this way. Better bored Angel than Angel amok. Still, I wish we could think of something that would pep him up, get him—"

She stopped in midsentence. Doyle had suddenly sat bolt upright and clamped his hands over his head. "What is it, Doyle? Do you have an idea?"

But Doyle shook his head, writhing in what looked like incredible pain, and she knew it wasn't an idea—it was a vision.

Doyle's visions, sent to him by the Powers That Be, were always of someone in trouble. Which meant there was something for Angel to do, she realized. Something to snap him out of his funk.

"A vision?" she asked. "Make it a good one, Doyle."

A moment later it passed, and Doyle released his head with a moan. "Oh, man, that hurts," he complained.

"Yeah, but could it have been any more nick of time-ish?"

Angel was suddenly in the doorway, looking at them.

"It walks," Cordelia said in a hushed voice.

"Did you have a vision?" Angel asked.

"A doozy," Doyle said. "Not a lot of detail, but plenty of background agony."

"I've rarely seen him looking quite so miserable," Cordelia added cheerfully.

"What's up?"

"I don't really know." Doyle massaged his own neck as he spoke. "Mostly what I got is a name and an address: Betty McCoy, 20047 Sunset, number 819."

"But you don't know what her problem is?" Angel asked.

"Not a clue," Doyle replied.

Angel glanced out the window and saw that it was growing dark outside. "Guess I'll go find out." He scribbled the address on a scrap of paper and stuffed it into his pocket.

"Anything you want us to do?" Doyle asked.

"Not till we know more about what's going on with Betty McCoy," Angel said flatly. "Just wait here. I doubt I'll be long."

He went out the side door and through his downstairs apartment to the carport where his 1968 Plymouth Belvedere GTX convertible was parked, and climbed in without opening the door.

At last, he thought, *a goal. An objective. Something real.*

Things had been quiet lately. Angel was torn between not wanting to wish something really bad on poor Betty McCoy, whoever she was, and hoping that her case was at least something interesting. Something to occupy his attention for a while. Even—though he hardly dared to hope it—something *different.*

He knew Doyle and Cordy thought he was bored. That wasn't the problem, really, but it was easier to let them think that than to try to explain what was actually getting to him. Sure, he was tired of the same old thing night in and night out. There wasn't much a person couldn't see and do in just over two hundred and forty years on the planet. The names and faces changed, and there was occasional new technology to spice things up, but for the most part, very little really changed. People still behaved in more or less the same old ways. Television was a modern variation on telling stories around the fire. Computer chat rooms were just a modern twist on the taverns and coffeehouses that had been around for centuries. The format was different, but not the real nature of the activity.

But there was more to his current mood than he'd let on to Doyle. He was starting to feel that he wasn't making a difference. Angel had spent the last hundred years trying to make up for the bad things he'd done in his first hundred and forty or so, but the harder he tried, the less sure he was that he could succeed. He'd saved countless lives—but maybe that was the problem. Saving the lives of people he knew was all to the good, but when one factored in the lives of people he'd never even met, people who would never even know they were in danger from some horror or other, the head count got a little vague. When he weighed the totality of his time on earth, it still looked as if the evil he'd done outweighed the good. And then there was the other concern—that it didn't really matter. That if he vanished from the planet tomorrow, before long those who had known him would have died off and he'd have left no mark at all, for evil or for good.

It was a disheartening revelation, and this, more than the boredom Doyle believed he felt, was responsible for his ennui. Boredom could be cured by activity. But what could he do about the other? How did one make an impact?

He could not worry about it tonight, though. He had Betty McCoy to worry about. He made it to Hollywood and hung a right on Sunset. Traffic was flowing smoothly, but Sunset had a lot of traffic lights and he seemed to get caught at every red one. *I hope Betty's problem doesn't involve any immediate deadlines,* he thought.

When he reached what he thought was the

address that Doyle had given him, he tugged the slip of paper from his pocket and checked it again. He was in the right place. He glanced up and down the street. He was definitely on Sunset.

With a shrug, he climbed out of the convertible and stood on the sidewalk in front of the wrought-iron gates to the Hollywood Peaceful Rest Cemetery.

Doyle's vision couldn't be wrong. The Powers That Be just didn't make that kind of mistake. Doyle could have recited the address wrong, transposed a couple of digits, but that seemed unlikely. The name and address were the whole vision, Doyle had said. They had still been fresh in his mind. He wouldn't have mixed them up.

Angel tried the gates. They were unlocked and swung open with a squeal that could have come straight from the sound-effects library of an old-time horror-movie studio. He passed through the gates, onto the cemetery grounds. A small guard-house, near the entrance, appeared to be empty.

Row upon row of headstones dotted a vast grassy plain that sloped gently uphill away from the entrance. Here and there larger or sculpted stones rose over the more standard ones, and occasional mausoleums towered over those. The cemetery was dark, only the moon and the faint light spilling over the tall fence from streetlamps on Sunset illuminating the grounds.

He didn't see anyone who looked like Betty

McCoy. He didn't see anyone at all. He started walking.

After a couple of minutes, a figure did come into view. But it wasn't any Betty McCoy, unless Betty was a fiftyish security guard with a gut that hung out over his belt buckle. This man was carrying a flashlight, and a billy club hung from his Sam Browne belt.

"Excuse me," Angel said hesitantly, when he drew close to the guard. "Is this place open?"

"Don't seem right to keep folks from seeing their loved ones," the guard replied. "We stay open till nine. The place is guarded around the clock, though."

Angel glanced at his watch. Just after seven-thirty.

"You looking for someone in particular?" the guard asked him.

"Betty McCoy," Angel said. "Number 819."

"Oh, Betty," the guard repeated with a smile. "She's right over here."

He knows her, Angel thought. *That'll make this easier.*

This was a strange place to find a woman in trouble, but people in trouble did some odd things.

He followed the guard up the path to where it crested a hill, and then down the other side. Three rows down, the guard turned off the main path and began walking across the grass. Angel continued to follow.

Then the guard stopped before a stone. Angel caught up to him. The guard clicked on his light, shone it onto the headstone. The stone was a small one with no unneccessary words on it.

"Elizabeth McCoy, 1939–1964," it said.

"Here's Betty," the guard told him. "Space 819. A guest of the state, looks like. You pay your respects. I'll be back toward the gate if you need anything."

"Thanks," Angel said.

The guard wandered away. Angel stood in front of the headstone for a few minutes, wishing that just once, one of Doyle's visions would be clear and simple.

Finally, he reached down and touched the cool stone with his fingertips. "Just let me know what you need, Betty," he said softly. "And I'll be there."

When she didn't answer, he headed back to his car, and home.

CHAPTER TWO

Some places have the names they deserve. Some are intentionally understated. And then there are those names, like the Rialto Lounge, that are vastly more exalted than the places themselves.

The Rialto Lounge had once deserved the fancy name, which was more than could be said for some joints. In the late fifties and early sixties, the heyday of what Joe Gagliardi liked to think of as the martini culture, it had attracted celebrities and working stiffs alike. The Rat Pack—Frankie and Dean and Joey and Sammy and the rest of them—had come in from time to time to listen to jazz and drink highballs while the commoners looked on. Cigarette and hatcheck girls wore outfits that highlighted cleavage over efficiency, and dreamed of meeting actors or producers or singers who could whisk them away to easy street.

Joe knew this from the clippings and photos that lined the wall behind the bar, not from personal experience. In the years since then, the club had been progressively diminished as one section of it after another was walled off and rented out to adult bookstores and massage parlors and a wig shop and a tattoo artist. Now it was an odd-shaped place, narrow at the doorway, wide at the back where the bar was.

Joe Gagliardi had been the evening bartender at the Rialto Lounge for thirteen years. He didn't love it or hate it. It was a job. He worked five days a week, got a week's vacation every year, took sick days when he needed them. He didn't make a lot of money, but he made enough to pay the rent on his apartment four blocks away, to keep gas in his 1977 Toyota Tercel, and to keep his freezer stocked with frozen dinners and his refrigerator with beer and sodas. On his vacation, he drove the Tercel down to a beach he knew in Mexico, on the Gulf Coast, and sat in the sun, fishing and drinking while his skin reddened and burned.

The hardest part of the job was probably listening to the same old stories again and again—drunks had a habit of repeating themselves, and pretty much nobody but drunks drank in the Rialto Lounge.

So there was kind of a sameness to Joe's days. He got up around eleven, shaved and showered, watched some TV and came to work at one in the afternoon. The day's hard-core drinking had already begun—it began when Lew opened the bar at six—but it was still quiet compared to the rush that came in after work, at five and again at six in the evening. Joe spent the evening serving beer from the tap and pouring shots and wiping the circles of condensation and spilled booze from the polished wooden bar, washing glasses and listening to sad stories of lost loves and grown-up kids and the one that got away. At nine, he threw his towel and apron into the dirty linens hamper and went home to heat up a frozen meal and sit in front of the TV until it was time to go to sleep and do it all again.

The night the stranger came to the bar was, until that moment, just like the one before it. Like the next one would be. But that night, at least, things were different.

He suspected as soon as the guy came in from the street that there was something strange about him. It wasn't just the clothes. The suit had narrow lapels and baggy slacks, the tie was thin and dark with three horizontal stripes, and the whole ensemble was topped off by a brown fedora that wouldn't have looked out of place in an episode of *The Untouchables*. But this was Hollywood, and if you judged people by their clothes, you were likely to tick off the next DiCaprio or Ribisi or Prinze. Or the current one.

So it wasn't just the clothes, though they were the first clue. It was also the guy's stance, the way he moved, the way he swaggered through the door like he owned the place, then turned at once toward where there had once been a checkroom but was now only a wall. People didn't come into the Rialto Lounge with that kind of attitude. People sneaked in, they slipped in as if they were ashamed to be there, or they staggered in, barely able to maintain their balance. It wasn't a place people came to be seen; it was a place they came to escape their lives, to look for oblivion in the bottom of a glass.

This guy looked to be in his mid-thirties. He was fit, and he was sober. His eyes were a clear, pale blue, and as he cased the room, it looked to Joe as if he was taking in and cataloging everything. His nose had been broken once or twice and set a little crooked. A cigarette perched on his lower lip.

When he saw nothing interesting where the checkroom had been, he turned back into the bar and walked straight to where Joe stood, drying glasses.

"You're not Bert," the man said, as if he had indeed expected Joe to be Bert.

"That's right, I'm not."

"Where's Bert?"

"Nobody works here named Bert. I don't think I even know a Bert, you want the truth."

"This is the Rialto Lounge, isn't it?"

"Sure is."

"Bert worked here nights, last time I was in."

"Well, he's not working here now."

The guy looked around again, scanned the area behind the bar as if Bert might be lurking just out of sight.

"So he's not. Where's the cigarette girl, then?"

Joe blinked a couple of times. "Cigarette girl?" he repeated with a snicker. "You can't even smoke in here, pal. In fact"——he slapped an ashtray onto the bar——"put that out before I get busted."

The guy looked confused, but he stubbed his smoke out in the ashtray. Joe scooped it up off the bar and emptied it. Most of the regulars were too far into their drinks to even notice the exchange, much less complain about the guy's smoking.

"Can't smoke in here?" the guy asked, seeming genuinely perplexed. "What kinda joint is this?"

"The Rialto Lounge, like you said."

"Doesn't look like it to me," the guy replied. "No checkroom, no cigarette girl, no bandstand. You even know how to mix a martini or a Tom Collins?"

"You want a beer and a shot, pal, I can set you up. You want anything much more complicated than that, you're on your own. And don't even talk to me about wine coolers or snappy Chardonnays or I might just have to take you outside and work you over."

The guy regarded him with those pale blue eyes.

"I think I like Bert better," he said. "What about Hal? You seen Hal around lately?"

"Hal who? Somebody else who don't work here?"

"Wechsler, you know. Hal Wechsler. Comes in here all the time."

"I don't know nobody name of Wechsler," Joe said.

The guy dug into a pocket and brought out a gold money clip holding some folded cash. He tugged a five-dollar bill out of the clip. He laid it on the bar, face up. Joe smiled down at Abe Lincoln as he swept his hand across the bill and made it disappear into his pocket.

"Still don't know Hal?" the guy asked.

"Still never heard of him."

The guy moved fast, his hand snaking out and catching Joe's shirt collar. He yanked down, and Joe's chin slammed into the bar. Holding him there, the guy put his face next to Joe's.

"Say, pal, I don't think I like you," he snarled through gritted teeth. "I don't think you're playing straight with me, see? I'm gonna give you a few seconds here to change your mind and stop talking nonsense. You follow me?"

"I . . . follow," Joe gasped. The man's fist at his throat was cutting off his breathing. "But I don't know these people you're talking about. Maybe you got the wrong place or something, I don't know. If I knew anything, I'd tell you."

The man released Joe with a hard shove.

"That's more like it," he said. He pulled a business card from his pocket, dropped it onto the bar. "You think of anything, you give me a call. Got it?"

"Right," Joe said. "I got it."

The man turned and walked out. Joe watched his back until he was gone, then picked up the business card and looked at it. In the center was a drawing of a large stylized eye. Above it was the name Mike Slade, and below it, the words "Private Eye," and a phone number with only five digits.

Joe rubbed his neck, glanced out around the drinkers. No one looked up. If any of them had even noticed, they were skillfully pretending they hadn't.

Mike Slade stepped outside and stood on the sidewalk, blinking in the light from a tall streetlamp just outside. He had known it would be a long shot that she'd still be working at the nightclub. Too many years had passed. It only took a glance into the newspaper boxes to see the date and know that. But some people got into a rut and stayed put for decades, and since it seemed like his best bet, he was hoping that had been the case here.

He glanced back over his shoulder at the faded sign. It said Rialto Lounge, all right, and it was just like he remembered it, fancy lettering and all, jutting out at an angle from the building, almost the way a sax player he'd known held his horn while blowing a solo. Except that the way he remembered it, the sign lit up, day and night, a flashing neon a guy could see from blocks away. But there was no neon in the sign now, though he could see the channels where it once had been.

Everything was different, and Mike Slade didn't like it.

The cars that cruised past on the street were all different, for one thing. They were small and boxy and strange-looking. He could recognize some of the makes—Ford and Chevrolet and the occasional Dodge—but not the models. Some of them didn't even look like cars; they were more like panel trucks, but sleek and with too many windows.

And the people inside them were different, too. They peered out of their cars with suspicious eyes, through windows that were sealed up tight as drums. Slade was used to people driving with their left elbow hanging out the window, a cigarette in one hand, using hand signals and waving to neighbors now and again.

Everything is different, he realized. *Everything. Not better, just different.*

Everything was different except him. He felt just the same. If his methods were outdated, then that was just the way it would have to be. The world had passed by while he slept, but he hadn't been there, and he couldn't change the kind of man he was.

He knew what had happened. He didn't know the how or the why of it yet, but he would. Answering questions was what a private dick did. And that was what Mike Slade was. A peeper. An eye. A private detective.

At least he had been until the day he was murdered.

He remembered that, too, every minute of it. November 12, 1961, a crisp autumn day. It had rained the night before, and the city was washed clean, sparkling in the sun when he walked to his office on Argyle from his apartment up on Hollywood Boulevard.

He'd whistled as he walked. The tune was Dave Brubeck's new hit "Take Five," he remembered. As he reached his building, after waving good morning to Lamont, who ran the newsstand on the corner, he segued into Bobby Darin's "Lazy River." Elvis Presley had released a couple of records already that year, but Slade didn't care for his kind of music. Unfortunately, it seemed to be catching on.

He pushed open the front door and said hello to Philip, the elevator man. Philip took him to the fourth floor. He inserted his key into the lock of suite number 411, and turned it. The knob turned easily—too easily.

Slade reached for his gun, but before it cleared his coat the door was yanked open from inside. Another guy barreled into him from behind, shoving him into the office. The door was slammed and locked, and Slade picked himself up, only to look down the barrels of two snub-nosed .38's.

"You been ignoring friendly warnings, Mac," one of them said, his voice dripping with menace. He was the one who'd been waiting inside. His black suit had narrow white stripes, and he wore it with scuffed brown loafers. He had blond hair cut close to the scalp. The other guy had dark hair, longer, and greased back. His suit was gray and baggy, but his black shoes were shined and tied.

"I don't take warnings from punks like Wechsler," Slade told them. "And you can tell him that if he has a message for me, he ought to deliver it himself."

"He's finished with messages," the blond man said.

"Yeah," the dark one added mirthfully. "Except for one last one. He told us to say good-bye." Then he opened fire.

Slade remembered the first couple of flashes from the gun barrels. He remembered a glimpse of Wechsler himself, stepping out from the corner where he'd been hiding. He was wearing something strange, a flowing black robe of some kind. But Slade didn't get a good look at it, and then he couldn't see at all.

He never did hear the shots.

Then nothing. Not even darkness, not silence, not the emptiness of the void.

It was almost as if no time had passed at all. But the moment he regained consciousness he knew it had. The moment his slumber was disturbed—when the people demolishing the building broke through the wall that kept him in.

At first the knowledge was terrifying. Slade understood that he had been dead but was dead no longer. He knew he had somehow violated the laws of nature, that he shouldn't be on the earth anymore.

He'd taken refuge in another vacant building nearby and stayed there, curled into a ball, listening to the noises, both strange and familiar, of Los Angeles. Hours had passed, he thought, before he realized that he could feel the cold of the cement floor seeping through his clothing. He ran a finger down the brick wall, savoring the sensation of the tiny irregularities of the stone catching at the skin of his finger. He tasted the brick, enjoying the dusty flavor on his tongue. His senses all seemed to work again.

He stayed there for the rest of the day, before he finally worked up the courage to come out. When he did exit his place of refuge, he spent some time trying to get his bearings. The garage where he'd parked his '58 Plymouth Valiant was now some kind of Chinese doughnut shop, so he figured the car was long gone.

In the end, it was Wechsler who had brought him out of hiding. Slade didn't know how long he'd been dead, didn't yet know what year it was. But if Wechsler was still alive in this strange future world, then he would have to pay for his crimes. Mike Slade was on a case, and Mike Slade never quit until his case was solved and his man was caught. He wasn't about to stop now.

But he needed a starting point. The trail had obviously gotten cold. If even the once-posh Rialto Lounge had gone to seed, then too many things had changed.

Veronica would be able to fill him in; he was sure of that. Veronica Chatsworth had been his secretary for almost seven years, since she was eighteen and fresh off the bus from Indianola, Iowa. He spotted a phone booth on a nearby corner and headed there, digging a nickel out of his pocket.

The phone booth looked like something out of a Flash Gordon movie. Still, the telephone had numbers—on buttons, not a dial, though the concept wasn't hard to figure out—and it had a slot for coins.

Only the writing over the slot said that a local call was thirty-five cents. It sounded like a scam to Slade. Lunch for thirty-five cents, he could see. A phone call ought never to cost more than a nickel.

And a nickel was all he had. He always carried one, in case he had to make a call. That and the bills in his money clip.

Slade left the booth, disgusted, and stood on Hollywood Boulevard until a taxicab came by. He waved and whistled, and the cabbie pulled over to the curb. Slade got in the back. The cabbie was a foreigner of some kind, with a name as long as Slade's arm. But when Slade gave him Veronica Chatsworth's address in Silver Lake, he nodded, smiled, and stepped on the gas. Slade sat back and watched the strange new world pass by.

CHAPTER THREE

Detective Kate Lockley stood in what was left of a building on Argyle Avenue in Hollywood, watching a couple of men from the coroner's office scrape what was left of a moldering skeleton into a body bag. It wasn't a pretty sight.

Charles Frezzano, the LAPD forensic technician assigned to the case, had spent hours examining the crime scene. The construction crew had called in their report, and the first officers on scene had secured the building. Kate caught the call for Homicide and showed up a few minutes later. Frezzano arrived about half an hour after she did.

There were plenty of places Kate would rather have spent the evening. This building had almost no windows left, and precious few walls. Downstairs, generators screamed and tall lights mounted on poles bathed the building in light, but Frezzano wanted the crime scene disturbed as little as possible, which meant only enough light to see clearly, and no heaters. She zipped up her soft leather jacket, tugged on gloves, and watched Frezzano do his slow, methodical search of the room.

After an hour of that, he yanked off his latex gloves and shoved them in his pocket, dismayed. "Crime's decades old, Kate. I'd put it at forty years, give or take. But the building has had people in it, off and on, ever since then."

"So there's no physical evidence left?"

"I'd never say there's none," he replied thoughtfully. He was in his fifties and had been with the coroner's office practically forever. Beneath a thick thatch of white hair his lean face was dominated by thick-lensed glasses in tortoiseshell frames. "But the law of diminishing returns does apply. I'm going to take a closer look behind that wall, because it's been sealed off as long as the body's been here. Once they move the body out of the way, I'll examine the space. Maybe I'll get some prints off the bricks."

"Worth a shot, I guess. What do you think you can get off the deceased?"

Frezzano looked at her over the tops of his thick lenses. "Well, cause of death, certainly. At a glance, I'd say we'll find that to be bullet wounds. Hopefully there'll be some lead in the mess inside that closet, or whatever it was."

"That would help," Kate agreed.

"No doubt. I wouldn't count on much more, though."

"Do you think you can get a positive identification of the victim?" she asked.

Frezzano stroked his chin with long, narrow fingers. "Possibly," he said without much enthusiasm. "There's no skin left on the fingers to take prints from. Dental records in the fifties and sixties weren't kept quite as reliably as they are today. And I'm assuming that the homicide took place sometime around then. But I'll narrow that down, and then we'll see where we are."

Kate turned in a slow circle, examining the room as if willing it to give up what it knew. "So what you're telling me, Charles, is that I've got a big fat goose egg."

He chuckled. "Kate, no one expects you to solve 'em all. Especially when they're forty years old."

"Says you."

"I'll give you a shout, let you know what I come up with. No need for you to stick around here."

"Thanks, Charles." She wished him good night and went down the stairs to her car, nodding to a couple of the officers who were securing the scene below. Even at this hour of the morning, a small crowd of onlookers had gathered, and a TV news crew was there with cameras, lights, and a reporter. *In Hollywood,* she thought, *it's all showbiz.*

The officers down here had detained the construction crew for questioning. These men and women had been here hours after they should have gone home. They'd been able to call their loved ones and change their evening plans, but until they gave their statements they were stuck here in Hollywood.

By now, most of them had been set free. One of the last to leave was a burly man named Blake, the site foreman who had called in the report. He was talking to a uniformed officer named Johannsen when Kate joined them.

"You're Mr. Blake?" she asked.

"That's right," the man said. His weariness sounded in his voice.

"I know it's been an inordinately long day for you, Mr. Blake," Kate said sympathetically. "I apologize for that."

"Not your fault."

"No, it's not. But I intend to find out whose fault it is. The blame, according to our forensic pathologist, lies about forty years in the past. The person you found upstairs was definitely the victim of a homicide."

"Sorry to hear that, ma'am." Blake's eyes were ringed and heavy from tiredness, but there was still a twinkle in them. His bushy mustache twitched as he smiled. "I wish I could help you, but I have to admit that I wasn't on this job site forty years ago."

"I'm sure you weren't even a gleam in your daddy's eye then," Kate replied. "But if you've noticed anything as you've been demolishing the building, I'd like you to try to remember it. If not tonight, then feel free to call me if anything comes to you. You might not think it's anything, but to us, trying to solve a case this cold, anything could be important."

"What kind of thing do you mean?" Blake asked.

"Could be anything," Kate said. She didn't mean to come across as vague, but there really was no telling what might be significant in a case like this one. She searched for specific examples. "A business card stuck in a doorjamb. A footprint made by someone stepping in the mortar of that bricked-up wall. Anything that might point us to someone who was here back then."

Blake shook his head slowly. "I'm sorry, ma'am," he said. His sadness seemed genuine. "I can't really think of anything like that. We've been spending our time tearing the thing down, you know, not looking for things we might want to remember about the place."

"Yes, I understand," Kate told him. She handed him her business card. "Please, if anything comes to you, don't hesitate to call me. Anything at all."

He took the card and tucked it into the breast pocket of his flannel shirt. "I'll do that, ma'am."

"Let him go," Kate instructed Johannsen. "Let them all go. But keep the place sealed up tight."

"You got it, Detective," the officer promised.

Kate took a quick last look around and headed for her car. Sleep would have been nice, but she had hours of desk work before that was an option.

Kate would head back to her office and pull missing persons reports from the time period that Frezzano had specified. She'd also get reports of any police activity at that building. Hopefully by cross-referencing between the two she could come up with some theory as to who the victim was and why he had ended up dead.

Cordelia looked up from her computer screen when Angel walked into the office. Doyle folded the newspaper he'd been reading and laid it on the couch.

"I've been researching Betty McCoy," Cordelia announced.

"Find anything?" Angel asked. He'd called from the road with news of the address.

"First of all, can I just say, ewww to the whole graveyard thing? I mean, what a creepy way to begin a case. I think maybe Doyle's vision machine is out of whack."

"There's nothin' wrong with me," Doyle protested. "I see what I'm supposed to see. No more, no less."

"Sure, whatever," Cordelia retorted. "Just not so incredibly helpful sometimes."

"Cordy," Angel interrupted. "Betty McCoy?"

"Right." Cordelia gave one sharp nod of her head. "Betty. There isn't much about her, but I was able to get a little from the *L.A. Times* archives. Did you know that at newspapers, they call the room where they keep all the old papers—"

"The morgue. Right," Angel said.

"Sorry. Continuing . . . Betty McCoy didn't make the paper very often, but there was a short article when she died."

"In 1964."

"Correct. She was, according to the paper, unemployed and addicted to drugs when she died. The only reason she made the paper, probably, was that she was alone in a hotel room, and it was four days before anyone found her."

"The housecleaning staff didn't go in?" Angel asked, incredulous.

"Not that classy a hotel, I guess. The reason they finally went in was that she was a couple of weeks late paying her bill, and they thought she had probably skipped."

"But she hadn't."

"No skippage involved."

"So we're lookin' at a penniless drug addict," Doyle said.

"Cheery, huh? Before she died, she worked as a cocktail waitress at a place called the Rialto Lounge."

"Hey, I've seen that place," Doyle said. "It's just off Sunset."

"Right. I get the feeling it's not what it was in its glory days, though."

"And Betty McCoy worked there in the glory days?" Angel asked.

"That's right," Cordelia replied brightly. "Dean Martin, Frank Sinatra, Ava Gardner—Hollywood royalty used to go there, according to another story I found. They weren't the every-night crowd, but they'd drop in. That made it a popular place for people who wanted to have a martini, listen to some cool jazz, and watch for celebrities."

"That ain't the Rialto I know."

"No, according to the article it started to go downhill in the mid-Sixties."

"And Betty lost her job?"

"I'm sure she wasn't alone in that. The article said the place was chopped up a couple of times. She was a cigarette girl. You know—the little tray of smokes at her waist, and the sexy outfit?"

"Glamorous," Doyle said. He didn't mean it.

"I know," Cordelia replied, with a faraway look in her eyes. She did. "I thought that kind of thing went out in the forties, though. The fifties didn't seem big on glamour, from what I've heard."

"They weren't," Angel told her. "They were a pretty conservative era. But in the early sixties, things changed. With John Kennedy's election and the passing of the Eisenhower era, a party attitude swept the country. Nightlife became important again. Music and dancing and dressing up were suddenly popular pursuits. In some ways it was like a return to the days you're thinking about."

"So the sixties weren't all hippies and marches and antiwar protests?"

"Not at all," Angel replied. "The first few years were really the last hurrah of that old-fashioned glamour."

"Sounds great," Cordelia said. "Men in tuxedos, women in pearls and sheath dresses—"

"So to sum up what we know about Betty McCoy . . ." Angel interrupted.

"Not much, is how I'd put it," Doyle offered.

"Not much is right," Angel went on. "She worked at this nightclub. She lost her job. Sometime in there she became addicted to drugs. She died poor and alone in a hotel room."

"That's pretty much it," Cordelia agreed.

"I don't get it," Angel said. "She had a miserable death. But what can we possibly do for her now? Why would Doyle have a vision about someone who's been dead for more than thirty years?"

"That, my friend, is the question of the hour," Doyle said. "If I'm gonna go through the pain, I'd prefer to do it for people who can actually be helped."

"You and me both," Angel said. "But let's not write this woman off yet. Someone needs to go back out to that cemetery, keep an eye on the grave." He looked at Cordelia and Doyle. There were no takers. He fixed his gaze on Doyle.

"Okay, I'll do it. But I hate cemeteries, Angel."

"You think I like them?"

"Well, you got that whole bein' dead thing goin' on."

"Not the same thing," Angel told him. "Cordy, how about if you keep looking into Betty's life? See if you can find out anything more about her or about that nightclub."

"Got it, boss. And you'll be where?"

"I'm going to go mingle with the royalty at the Rialto Lounge."

With an expression of abject horror, Mike Slade watched the numbers tick by on the cabbie's meter. Silver Lake wasn't that far from Hollywood—basically next door. He'd been anticipating a buck for the fare, another one for a generous tip.

So when the driver pulled up in front of Veronica Chatsworth's bungalow—which looked, in the glow from the streetlights, as if it hadn't changed a bit, except for maybe being in need of a paint job—and the fare was eleven dollars and change, Slade was irate. "This is highway robbery," he growled.

"The fare's the fare," the cabbie said, his accent thick. "I don't do nothing except drive the car."

"I think your meter's busted."

"No, I'm certain that it is not," the cabbie argued.

"Okay, fine," Slade relented. He peeled off twelve dollars, handed it to the driver. "Keep the change. Just don't let me see your face again."

The cabbie pocketed the bills and drove off into the night. Slade glanced over the house again. It stood on a quiet residential street. There were two square patches of dried-out grass with a sidewalk running up the middle, four steps, and a small porch that had a rusted metal glider on it. Slade remembered sitting on that glider, swinging back and forth, when it was brand-new from Sears Roebuck. He'd helped Veronica assemble it.

He mounted the steps and put his finger on the doorbell button, right where it had always been. *Some things,* he thought, *don't change.*

He pushed the button.

After a couple of minutes a porch light went on over his head, and the peephole in the door went black as someone peered out through it. He smiled at it.

"Who is it?" a female voice asked with some trepidation.

"Don't kid around, Veronica," he said. "It's me, Slade. Open up."

"Slade?" the voice repeated.

"That's right. Look, I know there's a lot to explain, so let me come in."

"Slade who?"

"Mike Slade. Come on, dollface."

He heard the sound of multiple locks being clicked open, and the door started to swing open. He reached for the knob.

"Just keep your hands where I can see them, Mr. Slade," the woman inside said.

He looked up at her. Not Veronica. Veronica was a statuesque green-eyed blonde; this woman was more compact and had rich dark brown hair, shoulder-length and pulled back into a ponytail, and level brown eyes that seemed to bore into him.

That, and a .38 special aimed at his midsection.

"Won't you come in?" she asked.

CHAPTER FOUR

The Rialto Lounge reminded Angel of a place he'd frequented as a young man, back in Ireland. He couldn't remember the name—believed, in fact, that it had no name. Nothing like a neon sign out in front, either. It had more or less been just a room in a stone building on a side street. One either knew what went on behind the closed door, or not. The first time Angel walked inside the place, he had been surprised and enchanted by it. The interior was cold and dank; the small fire flickering in a fireplace in one corner did nothing to dispel the chill. There were men all over the place, and a small handful of women. Big heavy mugs of ale were everywhere. There was loud laughter and rude comments and an occasional burst of song. But nearer the bar—two empty barrels with a plank on top of them—there was an air of desperation, and the people who drank there weren't at it to be sociable or to have fun, but to hide from their own existence. Those people, Angel thought at the time, were drinking themselves to death.

The Rialto Lounge had that same kind of atmosphere. It was a place where people drank because it was easier to pour themselves into their graves than to admit they were bent on self-destruction.

It gave Angel the creeps—and he was not, he knew, the easiest guy to creep out.

It was still early by the time he got there, not quite nine. The heavyset man behind the counter eyed Angel suspiciously when he walked in. He wore a stained white apron over a white shirt, the sleeves of which were rolled up to reveal thick, hairy forearms. A Band-Aid on his chin covered a bruise, but not well. He kept his narrow eyes on Angel all the way from the door to the bar. When he spoke, it was without welcome or humor. "Something?" he asked.

"Information," Angel said. Friendly guy, he thought. If he didn't work here, maybe he could get a job at the DMV.

"You must be confused," the bartender said, iceberg-cold. "This is a bar. You come here to drink. You want information, buy a newspaper."

"Okay, give me a beer," Angel agreed. He wouldn't drink it, but he'd pay for it and leave a tip, and maybe the guy would melt a little.

The bartender turned away from Angel, found a glass, stuck it under the tap. Amber liquid flowed into it. Then he set it down, hard, on the bar.

Angel slid a ten-dollar bill across the polished wood. "Keep the change," he said. The bartender went to the cash register, opened the drawer, and made some change. He stuck the change in his pants pocket.

"Busy night?" Angel asked.

"You bought a beer, not my undivided attention," the bartender replied.

Friendly *and* helpful. "I think I bought a little more than a beer."

The bartender regarded him coolly. "People think a lot of funny things."

"I'm trying to find out about someone who used to work here," Angel said. "Her name was Betty McCoy. I guess she was a cigarette girl."

The bartender's eyes narrowed further, and he ducked out of sight, looking for something kept underneath the bar. When he came back up, his pudgy hands were full of black metal.

A shotgun.

"Hold on," Angel said calmly. He held his hands up to show the guy he was unarmed. "Nothing to get excited about."

The bartender pointed the shotgun at the vampire. It wouldn't kill him, but its blast would certainly injure others. Behind him, Angel heard stools and chairs scraping on the floor as people rushed for the door.

Angel didn't want any of the patrons to be injured. They might not have been taking the best care of themselves, but a shotgun blast would finish the job in a sudden and painful way. He moved fast, slapping one palm down on the bar as a distraction and sweeping his other hand quickly, left to right, so when he caught the barrel it would not be dragged past his torso. His hand closed on the cold steel, and he pushed it safely to one side, where its blast, if it went off, wouldn't hit anybody. With the same motion he yanked it from the astonished bartender's hand.

"No guns," Angel hissed. He put the gun carefully on the floor at his feet, on his side of the bar, away from the bartender. "They make me nervous," he said with a quick smile.

"You're fast," the man said. He was still blinking at the speed with which Angel had reacted.

"Keep that in mind. Now, what's up? Why pull a shotgun on me?"

"I don't know what it is with you people today," the bartender said. "But the last guy asking about Betty McCoy got tough with me, and that's not gonna happen again."

"Someone else has been here asking about Betty McCoy?" Angel asked, surprised.

"I don't remember he mentioned her name," the bartender said. "But he asked about a cigarette girl."

"Today?"

"That's right."

"Tell me about it."

The bartender blinked again and glanced at the ceiling, as if the memory might be posted there. "It was early in my shift," he said. "Guy walks in wearing a weird outfit, like something out of an old movie."

"What kind of outfit?"

"Just a suit, you know, but old-fashioned. And one of those big hats nobody wears any more."

"Big hats," Angel echoed.

The guy waved his hands around his head, as if that would help paint the picture. "You know," he asserted. "Like in those gangster movies, when they all wore those hats. They'd get in these fistfights, and the hats would never come off."

"A fedora," Angel offered.

"Yeah, I guess so."

"Okay, so this refugee from an old gangster movie just walks in and asks about a cigarette girl who hasn't worked here since the sixties?"

"Well," the bartender paused, considering. "First, he asked about another bartender, named Bert. Only I've been here for thirteen years, and there's never been a Bert working here as long as I remember."

"Was he in the wrong place?"

"Not according to him. Said last time he was in the Rialto, Bert had this shift."

"Must've been a long time ago," Angel said.

"But the way he looked and acted," the bartender said, almost hesitantly, "was like it was yesterday. At least for him."

"How do you mean?"

"Well, you know, most people, if they haven't been to a joint in a couple of decades, they'll assume there's been some turnover in the staff. I mean, people are surprised I'm still here one night to the next. To be honest, so am I. But to walk in and just automatically think that the guy who worked behind the bar fifteen or twenty years ago or whatever would still be here . . . that's a little crazy, isn't it?"

"Sounds like it," Angel agreed.

"And the cigarette girl—we haven't had one of those in as long as I've been here, and I doubt that there's been one in the city of Los Angeles in twenty years. But if there had been, she wouldn't still be the same person."

"I see your point," Angel said. "More of a cigarette middle-aged woman."

The bartender nodded. "So the whole thing was pretty strange. But when I tried to tell him these people weren't here anymore, he got tough with me. Grabbed my collar, you know, slammed me into the bar. I was worried, I don't mind telling you. I keep the gun down here, but the way he was holding me, I couldn't get to it."

"So you can't tell me anything about Betty McCoy," Angel said.

"Never heard of her. If she's the girl this other clown is looking for, I wish her the best, but I hope I never hear of her again."

"What about employment records?"

"I actually thought about that," the bartender said, puffing up a little with self-importance. "Checked the file cabinet in back. But those files only go back to '86. There was a fire that year, I remembered. Most of the records were burned."

"Anything else you can tell me?" Angel demanded.

"You want the tough guy's name?"

"He told you his name?"

"He left me a card."

"Get it."

The bartender searched his pockets, then shook his head and went to the cash register. Stuck on top of the till was a rectangle of white cardboard. He picked it up, carried it back to the bar. "Here it is," he said. "Mike Slade, Private Eye." There was a phone number on it, but it was only five digits, preceded by "Hollywood." No area code. They hadn't used those phone numbers here for more than thirty years, Angel knew.

He picked the card up anyway. "I'll keep this," he said. "And trade you."

He put his own business card down on the bar. "If he comes back, or if anyone else comes looking for Betty, let me know immediately." He picked the gun up, cracked it, removed the shells, and put everything on top of the bar. "And by the way—a gun in this place? Bad idea."

He walked out into the Hollywood night.

There's just something about cemeteries, Doyle thought. *All those dead people under your feet.* He tried to stay on the paved walkways, figuring that the graves probably didn't extend under those. But there weren't very many paths. Most of the place was lawn, and whenever he walked on the grass he imagined skeletal hands grasping up through the earth, clawing at his legs.

He shivered. And not from the cold.

Doyle had been to a military graveyard once, and though he was saddened by all the death it represented, he found the order and structure somehow reassuring. All the stones were the same size, and they were neatly lined up in rows. The grass was carefully mowed. There were lots of flowers; splashes of red and yellow and pink among the white headstones left the impression that somebody cared.

Of course, that had been in the daytime.

But this place was closed. It was dark out. The witching hour had come and gone, but it was still hours before the sun would come up.

And frankly, he realized, being half demon didn't make him immune to the chills. Since meeting Angel, Doyle had seen lots of things he hadn't been exposed to before. Not all of them pleasant. Many of them related to the kinds of creatures who might come out of these graves . . . if in fact anything came out of the graves.

He was supposed to keep an eye on Betty McCoy's grave, in particular. And he was trying to. But he couldn't bring himself to just park himself in one spot and watch it. That left him feeling too . . . vulnerable, somehow. He wanted to keep moving.

In case I have to run, he found himself thinking.

This graveyard was more disturbing than some he had been to. He thought maybe it was the haphazard layout. Headstones of every size and shape stuck up out of the earth like exceptionally bad teeth. The grass around some of the stones, where a mower couldn't get in close enough, was long, and the blades whispered in the night breeze. The place was dark. And the fact that he was breaking the law and trespassing might have been a contributing factor, he realized.

Whatever it was, as the minutes ticked into hours, he felt more and more disturbed. He roamed the rows of stones, reading names and dates and epitaphs, the final visible remnants of hundreds of lives. He glanced over at Betty's grave every couple of minutes, waiting for . . . what, exactly? That was hard too, the not knowing. Remembering the vision and the headache that had followed it, but recalling also that the vision had been mostly notable in its lack of detail. He hadn't even had an image of her in his mind. Just her name and address.

Angel hadn't seemed too distressed by this place. But then, Angel was a vampire. And he'd been here during business hours. If Doyle ran into a guard, it was going to be bad.

So far, the only guard he'd seen had been in a guardhouse near the front, snoring in front of a portable television. That didn't mean the guy would stay asleep, though—some of those late night commercials were pretty loud, probably just for that reason. So he kept an ear cocked at all times for the jangle of keys on the guy's belt or the clack of shoes along the walkways.

It was a strange dilemma. He didn't want the guard to wake up, but at the same time, knowing there was someone else alive around the cemetery would be a good thing.

Doyle made one more circuit of the graves around Betty's, and waited for the sun.

CHAPTER FIVE

"So your name is Mike Slade?"

Slade was sitting on this woman's surprisingly comfortable brown sofa. The inside of the bungalow didn't look at all like it had the last time Slade had been here. But this woman clearly wasn't Veronica, so he guessed that shouldn't be a surprise.

Only one piece of furniture did look familiar—a huge leather chair Slade had bought, to sit in when he was visiting. The rest of the furniture was modern and uncomfortable-looking. A glass-topped black steel coffee table sat in front of the couch. A bookcase jammed with books leaned against one wall. There was a desk against another wall with something that looked almost like a little television on it, a white box around a dark screen. A couple of weeks' worth of newspapers were stacked up on the floor next to the desk.

The brown-haired woman was sitting in his

leather chair, and he didn't think it would be diplomatic to ask for it.

Especially since she still had the gun. And the way she held it gave the impression that she knew how to use it.

Slade had died once. He hadn't liked it much. He didn't know if he could die again. But he could feel. He had spent part of the evening enjoying the cool roughness of cement, the slickness of glass, the sharp edge of a brick corner. So whether he could die or not, he figured a bullet would hurt.

"That's right," he said. "A woman who once lived here used to work for me. Her name was Veronica Chatsworth."

The brown-haired woman smiled. "You're going to have to do better than that," she said. "Although I do like the suit. Nice touch."

"Meaning what?" he asked.

"I know who Veronica Chatsworth is," she said. "And I even know who Mike Slade is. Was. But first of all, he's dead. And second, if he wasn't dead, you'd be about forty years too young to be him."

"You know Veronica?" he asked. *A lucky break*, he thought. "She can vouch for me."

"I *knew* her very well," the woman said, her voice suddenly distant. "She's my mother. She's dead too."

Slade paused, choosing his words carefully. "I'm really sorry to hear that," he said. "She was a terrific lady."

"Thanks. She maybe could have been a better mom, but I loved her."

"You're not the only one," Slade said softly.

"So don't come in here telling me you're someone you couldn't possibly be," she said, her voice suddenly shrill with anger. "I don't want to listen to that. I won't."

"Just hear me out," Slade beseeched her. "Please."

"You have five minutes," she said. "Don't waste them, because there are no extensions."

Slade dived right in. "I don't know any way to convince you that what I'm going to say is true. But it is. Every word of it. Before I get into it, though, can I ask your name? I like to know who I'm talking to."

"I'm Barbara Morris," she said. "LAPD. Want to see my shield?"

"I'll take your word," he replied, though he was astonished that a woman could be a police officer in this strange future. Another thought, frightening in its implications, popped into his head. "This will sound strange, but can you remind me what year this is, Barbara?"

"What year? Have you been skipping your medication?"

"Humor me," he said.

She told him the year. What she said jibed with the date he'd seen on a newspaper, and he heaved a sigh of relief. She was too young. Any daughter of his would be almost forty, and this young lady wasn't more than twenty-five. "I am Mike Slade. I did know your mother. Now, this is the part you're not going to believe—I've been having a hard time with it myself. I was dead. I was murdered in 1961. But here I am. I can't explain it."

"Did I say five minutes?" Barbara Morris asked. "I meant five seconds. Get out."

"Please," Slade said quickly. "Veronica had a little mole on the back of her neck. She put makeup on it sometimes, to hide it, but it was there." He pointed to a doorway leading out of the living room. "Through there is the room that used to be her bedroom. The curtains were red-and-white check, like the tablecloth at an Italian restaurant. She had a big cedar chest at the foot of her bed that she used to sit on to take her shoes off. She always lined her shoes up carefully next to it."

"Okay, you knew her. Or you've done some research. What about it?" Barbara demanded.

"What kind of research would tell me something like that?" Slade asked. "Would research tell me that she hated to be tickled or that she was shy about the thickness of her ankles? She was a great-looking lady, but she always wore long dresses or slacks in those days."

Barbara Morris glared angrily at him. "I don't know where you're getting this stuff, but—"

"It's true, isn't it?"

"What if it is? It doesn't mean that you're—"

"Did she ever describe Mike Slade to you?"

"No, she . . . she didn't have to."

"What do you mean?" he asked her.

"I mean . . . there's a picture. Wait here." She waved the gun in his direction. "I mean it. Do not move from that spot."

He held up his hands. "I'm not budging."

She disappeared through the door, the one that had led to Veronica's bedroom. He heard her rummaging around, probably in the closet, opening boxes, it sounded like. In a few minutes she came back with a black-framed photo in one hand, the .38 in the other.

Oh, that one, he thought. He remembered the photo. It had been taken at the Pacific Ocean Park, in '57 or '58. They'd been enjoying a day in the sun, going on rides, eating cotton candy. Late in the day, as the sun slipped toward the Pacific and their shadows stretched long toward the east, they came across a booth where you could get your picture taken in silly costumes—old West clothes, flapper outfits, and the like. They picked a sheikh and a harem girl. Slade sat down in a big wicker chair, and Veronica stood behind him, her hands on his shoulders. He'd had to come back the following week to pick up the print.

"It's a couple of years old," he said.

"More than a couple," she replied. "But I have to say, it does look like you."

"That's because it is. We were at Pacific Ocean Park. At the pier in Santa Monica."

"So you're saying that you're Mike Slade, the P.I. my mom worked for. And you were also sweeties? And then you were killed, but now you're back."

"I know what it sounds like, ponytail, believe me."

"I'm not sure you do."

"It sounds crazy," he assured her. "I know that. It's crazy for me, too, you have to believe that. I mean, the last time I saw Los Angeles, it was 1961. Kennedy was president, Cuba belonged to the commies, and everyone was going to see *West Side Story* at the movie theaters. Someone gave me a book called *Thunderball,* about a spy named James Bond. You ever heard of that?"

"Ian Fleming. He's dead too."

"You're gonna get me depressed, you keep telling me who's dead."

"I don't suppose you heard about Kennedy?" she asked.

"Him too?"

Barbara nodded. "Assassinated. November twenty-second, 1963."

Slade shook his head sadly. "So LBJ finally got to the White House?"

"For a while."

"This sounds insane, I know that," Slade told her. "But I swear to you, every word of it's true. I can show you my private investigator's license."

"Does it have a picture?"

"No."

"Let's see it anyway," she said cautiously. "But careful with the hands. Anything comes out of your pocket that's not a wallet or a license case, I shoot. And I have some marksmanship medals."

"Don't look like a marks*man* to me."

She gave a short laugh. "That's the first thing you've said that sounds like what Mom told me about Mike Slade."

He reached into his inside jacket pocket and, with two fingers, withdrew the leather case he carried his license in. He handed it to Barbara Morris. She flipped it open, studied it.

"Looks authentic," she said.

"Because it is. You've seen the license, you have the picture. I don't know how else to convince you."

"I don't either, because it's just too unbelievable. I'm supposed to accept that I'm sitting here talking to a dead man?"

"Yeah, I wouldn't buy it either."

"So tell me this, Casper. What brings you here? What did you want with my mother?"

"It's kinda scary for me too, waking up dead. Everything is so different. You know what a phone call costs in a pay phone now?"

"Yes."

"Of course you do. But it was a shock to me, I gotta tell you. So I thought maybe Veronica could help me make sense of things. She was always good at that. When I was stumped, I could just talk things out with her and she'd show me what I was missing."

"Sounds like Mom."

"She's the best. She could also stir a mean martini. I'm wondering if you inherited that skill."

Barbara Morris looked flatly back at him, so he went on. "But anyway, when I was killed, I was working on a case. I'm sure that my death had to do with that case, and I'm sure that the reason I'm back is that I never solved it. I never brought the guy in, even though I knew who it was. I never got the goods on him. And then he got me. I figure I'm back so I can bring him down."

"How noble," Barbara said, a sharp edge to her voice.

"Nothing noble about it, but it's my job, and if a man doesn't do his job, then what kind of guy is he?"

"My dad was like that," Barbara said.

"Your dad was a private eye?"

She shook her head. "Cop."

Slade chuckled. "Veronica married a flatfoot. Go figure. That why you're a cop?"

"I'm not yet, actually. I'm in the Academy, though."

"I'm still amazed women can wear slacks on TV, and you're in the Academy," he said incredulously.

She buried her face in her hands, the barrel of

the .38 pointing at the ceiling. "I just can't get my mind around this," she said. Then she parted her hands, looked at him. Examined him, like a butterfly pinned to a board. "I mean, you look authentic. You sound authentic. Like you're genuinely surprised that women can be police officers."

"I'm surprised women can *date* police officers," he said. "Cops I've known—"

"Well, if you are who you say you are, you'll find that things have changed. A lot."

"You don't have to tell me that. You ever hear of a style of music called rock and roll?"

"Sure."

"It died, right?"

"You were hoping it would?"

"I was convinced. Why?"

"Bad news, I'm afraid."

An hour later they were sitting at a wooden table in the dining room. Slade thought he'd convinced her— at least, as far as he could tell, since he still wasn't entirely convinced himself. But he'd been telling her stories about her mother, and they'd laughed together. For a few minutes she had cried. She had put the gun away and brought out a photo album Veronica had started in the early sixties. It contained a few more pictures of Slade, and many photos of Vic Morris, the man she eventually married.

After they closed the album, they sat quietly at

the table for a few minutes. To break the silence as much as anything, he spoke up.

"So did she just close up the office after I was killed?"

"Not that I know of," Barbara said. "Remember, I didn't come along for quite a few years. She told me the story, though. How she kept going to work for a couple of weeks, sure you were just undercover somewhere and would get in touch. But you didn't. The rent came due, and she paid it out of her savings. Still no word from you. By the time the next rent came, she'd been living off her savings, since she wasn't getting a paycheck. There were other bills—lights, phone. She finally came to accept that you were dead. Or that you'd show up in five years with some incredible story. But you never did, so she finally got on with her life."

"She ever mention a girl named Betty McCoy?"

"Not that I remember. Why? Who's she?"

"My last client. The one I got killed trying to help."

Barbara just looked at him for a moment, and he couldn't read her expression. "What?" he finally asked.

"You say that so matter-of-factly."

"That I got killed? Believe me, it's not easy to get used to. But I can't really deny it either, if you know what I mean. It's not like I went to sleep in 1961 and woke up now."

"I suppose not," she agreed. "So your intention is to finish this case you were working on? And then what?"

"Way I figure it, once Wechsler is in stir, I'll probably go for good. Get the rest I'm supposed to have."

"Wechsler? That's the guy who capped you?"

"If by that you mean shot me, yeah. Mug name of Hal Wechsler."

Barbara stared into space for a moment. "Hal, as in Harold?" she asked.

"Could be, yeah. I think so. You know him?"

"I know *of* a Harold Wechsler, I think. Wait here."

She went into the living room for a moment, then returned carrying a newspaper. She folded the long pages back and handed it to Slade. "That look like him?" she asked.

He studied the picture. It was a grainy black-and-white photo of two men shaking hands in front of a large DWP banner. Both were middle-aged white men with thinning hair. The one who was supposed to be Harold Wechsler had a narrow pointed nose, high cheekbones, and wide-set eyes.

Hal Wechsler had had those same features. Less weight, more hair. But a lot of time had passed since Slade had last seen Hal Wechsler. A lot of time for Wechsler, anyway. For Slade, it seemed like almost no time had passed, like he'd seen Wechsler yesterday.

"That's him," he said. "What's he doing here?"

"That other guy is the mayor of Los Angeles," Barbara explained. "He's just appointed your friend Wechsler general manager of the Department of Water and Power."

"You mean Wechsler's in charge of all the juice for the city?" Slade was aghast. "He's a small-time crook."

"The electricity *and* the water supply. Not a small job, in a city that's basically desert. Looks like he's not so small-time any more."

"But he's still a crook," Slade insisted.

"People can change. Forty years is a long time, Mr. Slade. He could have turned over a new leaf, become a legitimate businessman."

"Has water in L.A. ever been a legitimate business?" Slade asked.

She smiled. "You got me there."

"May I have this picture?"

"Be my guest," she said. Slade ripped the photo from the newspaper, folded it once, and slipped it into the inside breast pocket of his jacket.

"I have to go," he announced.

"Listen, Mr. Slade. I'm sort of coming to accept your story, bizarre as it sounds, because you do seem so much like the guy my mother told me about."

"Nice she still talked about me."

"You'd be surprised. So anyway, I want you to be careful. I know you're already dead, or you think you are anyway. But still—I don't know, just be careful. And don't do anything stupid."

"Like what?"

"Like seek revenge, for one thing. You can't just go shoot this guy Wechsler. I'd hate to see you in trouble with the law."

"Ponytail, private eyes are always in trouble with the cops. It's just the nature of the game."

"Used to be, maybe. Things change. Even that."

"I'll believe it when I see it." Slade rose, pushed the chair back into place under the table, and headed for the door. Barbara followed him there. He opened it, and she held on to the inside knob.

"It's funny," she said, a little wistfully. "I almost feel as if I know you."

"I wish I'd had the chance to know you," he replied. "Maybe when all this is over, if I'm still around . . ."

"Yeah, maybe. You be careful out there, Mike Slade."

"I promise." He closed the door.

Barry Fetzer and Harold Wechsler got out of Wechsler's limo in front of the Argyle Avenue demolition site. A bored-looking cop was standing in front of the fence, arms crossed over his chest. He gave them a curious look when they approached.

"We'd like to get into the building," Wechsler told the cop.

"Sorry, sir. This is a crime scene. No admittance."

Wechsler pulled out his wallet, showed the officer his identification. "My name is Harold Wechsler," he said. "I'm general manager of the Department of Water and Power."

"This building doesn't have either one, that I'm aware of," the cop told him.

"But the new construction will. I just need to take a quick look around."

The police officer's name was Deke Johannsen. He'd been on the force for seven months. He'd joined to catch lawbreakers, keep the city safe from crime, all that. Standing guard outside construction sites wasn't in the job description, as far as he was concerned.

But one thing he knew, making friends with political bigwigs could only be a good thing.

He opened the gate.

Barry Fetzer clicked on his Maglite and led the way up the stairs. When they reached the fourth floor, Wechsler took the flashlight and led Fetzer down the hall to an office. He walked with confidence, even in the cluttered dark, as if he came here every day.

A moment later they stood in front of a closet with a largely demolished brick wall behind it. Wechsler played the light over the inside. Fetzer tried to read his boss's body language. The man was angry, wound tight. His shoulders were hunched, his arms rigid.

"It's too late," Wechsler said at last. "Way too late."

"Listen, Hal," Barry began. "I'm sorry. They wouldn't let me—"

"I don't want to hear your excuses, Barry," Wechsler growled. "I sent you to deal with this situation before things went wrong. There were ways we could have prevented this from being a problem."

"I know. I was ready. I had that water you gave me to sprinkle on the wall. I knew the words to say. But I couldn't get in."

"I should have done it myself," Wechsler said wearily. "I should have known better. It's on me, Barry."

"Yeah, well, I'm still sorry. I tried."

They started back down the stairs, Wechsler still carrying the flashlight. "I know, Barry," he said almost sadly. "And by the way, after I get into the limousine . . ."

"Yeah, boss?"

"Kill that cop. Leave no witnesses."

CHAPTER SIX

Los Angeles City Hall soars twenty-eight stories over Main Street. When it was built in 1926, the building code didn't allow buildings more than twelve stories tall, so a special waiver had to be passed for City Hall. It towered over its neighbors, and is still an imposing structure.

But those who worked in it every day, like Franklin Griffith, grew accustomed to it before long. Griffith was a nine-year police department veteran assigned to guard duty in City Hall's lobby. He felt most days like the guy in the airport who takes people's keys and watches as the carry-on bags go through the X-ray machines. His post was one of the metal detectors that all visitors to the building had to pass through, in these high-security, low-trust times.

Most days, he worked with Mark Barrow, another

longtime cop. Barrow was an okay guy, but he was a little short-tempered and liked to complain about anything and everything. A cop met all kinds on the job. Franklin had been partnered with people he had nothing in common with and with others who might have been family, and after a while, they were all the same. A police officer trusted brothers-in-arms more than civilians, and that was just the way it was. The men and women in uniform were the ones Franklin wanted at his back.

Not that he needed anyone at his back on this gig. Sometimes he had to open a briefcase or a purse, because a metal cigarette case or a tin of breath mints set off the detectors. Usually the people carrying these items were no more dangerous than Franklin's grandmother, who cringed when she had to shoo a fly.

So it was a trade-off. Not the kind of job that was going to put his life in mortal danger. But also not the kind that impressed ladies or led to a promotion or even to an interesting conversation.

Franklin took up his position beside the metal detector and nodded to Barrow, who was checking out a city employee's laptop computer. Another day on the job.

Mike Slade looked at the City Hall building. It had hardly changed, though the neighborhood around it had changed considerably. Buildings had shot up into the sky far beyond the height he had thought they'd reach on this coast. Slade had been to New York years before—well, everything he had ever done was years before now, he realized. This constant adjusting of his own personal timeline was becoming a chore.

In New York he had been impressed by the height of the Chrysler Building and the Empire State Building. He remembered standing on Fifth Avenue looking up at the expanse of steel and glass of the Empire State and thinking that it really could snag a drifting cloud. He was sure he was seeing the peak of human ingenuity, that nothing would ever be built to rival that construction.

Los Angeles, on the other hand, had been timid about tall buildings. California was earthquake country, and builders forgot that at their peril. The buildings in downtown L.A. now didn't come close to the Empire State Building in height, but they were still stratospheric compared to what Slade was used to. He felt like a rube, standing here on the sidewalk craning his neck to look up at them all.

Besides, the guy he was after was holed up inside City Hall somewhere. He tapped the comforting weight of his Browning .38 and went on in.

Slade tugged at his suit, trying to look like any of the other city government workers who were filing inside. Just through the doors, people narrowed to a single line to walk through something that looked like a plastic doorway, except that there was no door in it. Set up next to it was a conveyor belt that passed inside a big box-like structure and came out the other side. The belt was operated by a short woman who didn't look as if smiling came easily to her. Next to her there was a cop, and another one stood by the crazy doorway.

Slade got in line, and after a few moments, stepped through the doorway.

And the doorway began to beep loudly.

"Sir," one of the cops said. "Please step back and walk through again."

"What is this thing?" Slade asked.

"It's a metal detector, sir. Please step back through and try again."

"What, it doesn't work backward? What if I turn around and back through next time?"

The cop looked as if he had run out of patience before he even came to work this morning. Slade stepped back through the doorway. When he was clear of it, it stopped beeping. A small crowd had gathered around, watching him.

He walked through the doorway again.

It beeped.

The cop picked up something that looked like a wand and aimed it at him. "If you'll just step over here, sir," he said.

Slade unbuttoned his jacket. "If it's a metal detector, it's probably just picking up my gat," he said, reaching inside. His hand closed around the grip and he drew the pistol out.

"He's got a gun!" someone behind him shouted. There were screams, and panicked footfalls.

"Drop it!" the cop shouted. He drew his own weapon.

"It's okay," Slade said. "I'm a private eye. I'm licensed to carry it."

"Drop it!" the cop repeated angrily.

Slade aimed his gun at the cop. "You drop it," he said.

"Drop the weapon," a voice behind Slade said. The second cop, no doubt. He was probably aiming his gun at Slade's head.

Slade figured that one of two things could happen: He was already dead, so the bullet might just pass harmlessly through him and into the cop standing in front of him. There would be a certain pleasure in that—private eyes and cops were lifelong rivals, and Slade had been shaken down by enough dirty ones to glean a sliver of enjoyment from the idea of a cop taking a bullet meant for him. But the other possibility was that he had been brought back to real life, not to some strange half-life, and a bullet entering his skull would burn and cause incredible pain before it killed him all over again.

Considering the options took less than a second. Weighing his responses took another one: He could drop his gun. But then there would still be two armed cops, and he'd be defenseless. He had no illusions about cops—they'd as soon deal with a P.I.'s corpse as with the P.I. himself. So the best plan seemed to be to get out of this situation, with his gun, and try for Wechsler some other way.

"I don't suppose it'd help if I told you I was here to arrest a murderer," he said.

"Drop it now!" the first cop demanded.

"Gotcha, pal," Slade said, keeping his voice low and even. He acted as if he was lowering the weapon to the floor, beginning to bend from the waist. What he was really doing was reducing the size of the target he presented. At the same time that he bent, he turned sideways to both cops, increasing the likelihood that they'd miss him and hit each other when the fireworks started.

When he saw the cop in front of him exhale and start to relax, he fired.

He aimed for the guy's arm—and he always hit what he was aiming at. The .38 made a huge booming sound that echoed through the lobby. People screamed, including the cop, whose forearm jetted blood where Slade's bullet ripped into it. The cop's piece went flying, hitting the tiled floor twenty feet away and clattering into a wall.

At the same instant that he fired, Slade spun and ran for the doorway. He heard someone—probably the second cop—call "Stop!"

Which, of course, Slade did not do.

He ran all the faster, grabbing people as he went. They shied away from him, but the entryway was too crowded for everyone to avoid him. He wanted just to tag them as he passed, to make sure the cop understood that Slade was in contact with civilians at every step. This would ensure that the cops wouldn't fire on him.

In a moment he was outside in the glorious Los Angeles sunshine.

And he could hear sirens coming toward him from every direction.

Of course! he thought. *The Police Administration Building is only a block away. One quick call and every flatfoot in town would be on the way over.*

He turned and ran up West Temple, away from the P.A.B. Over the sound of his own footsteps pounding the pavement and the blood rushing in his ears, he could hear the sirens getting closer. Most of the squad cars were turning onto Main and heading for the City Hall doors.

But not all of them.

He poured on the heat. There were a few people on the sidewalks, but he dodged them as he ran, and most of them didn't seem to connect him with the sounds of pursuit.

Two blocks up was Broadway, and he hung a sharp right. Broadway was always crowded, and Slade figured he'd be able to hide among the people there. Today was no exception. The sidewalks were jammed with people of every description, every color. Two older women with paper shopping bags in either hand stepped out of a bodega, and Slade nearly collided with them. But he sidestepped, and went around them, only to hear them cursing him fluently in Spanish as he went past.

The sirens kept shrieking up West Temple.

Safe. He slowed to a walk, stepped off Broadway into a store, and browsed for a while. A candy bar sounded good, so he located the candy rack, and almost fell over at the range of choices.

And then the prices.

A buck for a chocolate bar?

There were some definite disadvantages to waking up in this time period. Maybe everyone was now a millionaire, but he only had what was in his pocket, and he doubted he'd be able to hang out a shingle after this.

On the other hand, he didn't think he'd need long-term funds. Just enough to carry him until he brought down Hal Wechsler. After that, he really would be just a memory.

Franklin Griffith sat in an interview room in Parker Center three hours later, his arm in a sling and a brace. The bullet had shattered his wrist, and the doctor wasn't sure he'd ever get the full use of it back. But the suspect who'd shot him was still at large, and the only hope of tracking him down was for Franklin and Mark Barrow to give detailed descriptions, try to get a computerized portrait done that could be passed out to the officers on the street.

Franklin sat behind a table, cradling his arm with his good hand. A detective named Benny Shimoto sat on the other side, giving him a sympathetic look.

"It hurt much?" Benny asked.

"Like crazy." Franklin tried on a smile, but it didn't fit and he lost it.

"That really stinks, man," Benny said.

"You're telling me."

"Are you sure you're up to this? We've already got Barrow's statement."

"I think I got a better look at the guy," Franklin replied. "He was facing me when he fired the gun."

"Good point," Benny agreed. He took a sip from a white mug with coffee stains running down the sides like paint on a can. Franklin was washing down aspirin with a soft drink. "So what can you tell me about the shooter?"

Franklin searched his memory. "Mid-thirties, I'd say. Caucasian. Brown hair, blue eyes. Six feet tall, one-eighty or so."

"Sounds like a lotta guys."

"Yeah, I know. There wasn't much about him that was special in any way. Except his clothes."

"What about his clothes?" Benny asked, intrigued.

"They were about thirty years out of date," Franklin explained. "He was wearing a baggy suit, kind of boxy-looking, you know. But not the way baggies are today. It was a flat gray that you don't see much anymore. And he had one of those hats on, like Humphrey Bogart or something. Real old-fashioned."

"What about his weapon?"

Franklin slapped his forehead lightly with his good hand. "I should've thought of that," he said. "It was old. Real old. Looked like an old Browning, a .38 snub-nosed. I knew something seemed strange about it, but I was too busy getting shot with it to give it much thought at the time. Was the slug recovered?"

"No slug. And it's not inside you, according to the docs."

"That's what they tell me," Franklin agreed. He'd have shrugged, but that would have hurt too much. "Shell casing?"

"Not that either," Benny told him.

That was strange, Franklin thought, but he didn't say anything to Benny. The detective probably had his own ideas. The shooter had no time to collect his own slug or his shell. Must have been some souvenir-hunting civilian, he figured, who didn't understand that he or she was walking away with vital evidence.

"Think you can sit still for a composite?" Benny asked.

"I should do it while it's fresh in my mind," Franklin said. "I want to make sure we get this guy."

"He shot an LAPD officer in our own City Hall, a block from Parker Center," Benny assured him. "We'll get him. Don't you worry about that."

"I know we will," Franklin said. "With any luck, I'll be there when we do."

Benny shook his head. "You'll be on disability for a while," he said. "But you'll testify at his trial."

Franklin finally smiled. "That's good enough for me," he said. "Let's go draw a picture."

CHAPTER SEVEN

Kate Lockley sat at her desk staring at the computer-generated photograph.

There's no way this makes sense, she thought. *No way at all.*

It was making her head hurt, but she couldn't stop trying to puzzle it out.

On one side of her desk lay an old file photo of a private detective named Mike Slade, who had disappeared in the early sixties. He had rented the office space on Argyle Avenue in Hollywood where a corpse had turned up that was, according to the coroner, just old enough to be Slade.

On the other side of the desk was a computer printout of a composite picture made from the descriptions of two police officers, one of whom had been shot and wounded at City Hall. This picture showed their version of the shooter.

The shooter had been described as wearing clothes that looked at least thirty years out of date.

The two pictures could easily have been of the same man.

It just doesn't fit, Kate thought. *How can a guy who vanished in 1961 be back—and not a day older?*

Then there was an additional problem. Kate had been awakened that morning—very early that morning, after having had very little sleep—by an urgent message. She had to get back to the Argyle address right away: There was another body.

And this one was a cop. A cop who had been alive just hours before. The one, in fact, that Kate had assigned to keep the crime scene buttoned down. His name was Deke Johannsen.

She drove to the scene. Identified the body and watched it get zipped into a black rubber bag and taken away.

Then she and Deke Johannsen's captain drove out to his parents' home in Alhambra—he wasn't married, but he had his parents and a younger brother—and reported his death to them.

The Johannsens lived in a single-story ranch house with pink stucco walls. Deke's father was a big man, a former marine who worked as a bus mechanic for the L.A. Department of Transportation. His mother worked part-time as a motel maid. She was a Russian émigré whose English was heavily accented. When the captain explained what had happened to their son, tears began to roll soundlessly down the father's cheeks. The mother sat totally still, not betraying the slightest hint of the emotion she must have been feeling. After a few moments, she put one hand on her husband's massive shoulder and squeezed it.

Kate had seen this before. Despite common beliefs, men were often the emotional ones, women the strong ones who provided the steady foundation on which families were built. In this family, Deke's mother was the rock.

After spending thirty minutes with the Johannsens, Kate and the captain had driven back to Parker Center, not speaking the whole way.

This was the part of the job she hated most. She understood that being a police officer carried a certain amount of risk, that the mortality rate was considerably higher for a cop than for your average civilian. She was prepared to accept the fact that she might someday die in the line of duty. But when someone else died, she took it hard. Especially if, as in this case, it was she who put that someone into the line of fire. It hit her in the gut, tied her into knots. She figured she wouldn't be much of a cop if it didn't.

That was what kept her in Homicide. She wanted to find murderers and put them away so they couldn't kill again. Ideally, she would make herself useless, obsolete. The city would become so safe there would be no need for homicide cops.

Never happen.

But the ideal drove her, kept her going. Even when she faced something as seemingly impossible as the case of the dead P.I.

Mike Slade had been dead since 1961. He had died in his own office building on Argyle Avenue. Today he had shot and wounded a cop. He could have shot to kill, but he didn't—or was he just a lousy shot, even at close range?

Did he kill Deke Johannsen?

Survey says yes.

Not everything added up, of course. Things rarely did, so early in the game. Johanssen had been shot once in the back of the skull with a 9mm slug. Franklin Griffith had, according to the reports, been shot with a gun that was at least thirty years old. Which jibed with the idea that the dead detective, Slade, was carrying it around. But no physical evidence, no slug or shell casing, had been found to back up those reports. Griffith's wound, according to the doctor, was consistent with a .38 caliber round.

So was he carrying two guns? And why, if he was an old-time private eye from the sixties—or masquerading as one, which seemed more likely— would he also carry a 9mm?

So many questions. So few answers.

She looked again at the file she'd pulled on Mike Slade. He'd rented the office for almost ten years and had been renting it at the time of his disappearance. He had a longtime secretary named Veronica Chatsworth. He had never married. He was a fixture in the Hollywood scene of the late fifties and early sixties, working for studios on occasion and for small-time actors when he could. He'd even served as a technical adviser for a while on a TV series called *77 Sunset Strip*. He had developed a bit of a specialty digging up dirt for actresses who wanted to divorce their husbands, back in the days before no-fault divorce became state law.

He was considered tough, potentially dangerous, and very good at his job. He had closed some major cases that the LAPD hadn't been able to solve, including the high-profile murder of newspaper publisher Oswald Sternwood in '56. But he'd never had good relations with the police. He'd been on the force very briefly in the early fifties and been fired during a police corruption scandal. From what Kate could tell from skimming the file, he didn't seem to be involved in the corruption, but he had turned up evidence that implicated three of his superior officers, and they had fired him before they were indicted. After their convictions, the department had offered to reinstate Slade, but he had already taken a P.I. license and started lining up clients. He apparently never looked back, but he never forgot his treatment at the hands of the department, either.

There wasn't much to go on in the file. She decided to check with some of his former clients to see if she could turn up anything on Veronica Chatsworth.

Before she started down that road, though, she wanted to talk to someone else about the case. Someone who knew a little about private investigators and a lot about weird.

"So what have we learned about Betty McCoy?" Angel asked. Cordelia sat behind her desk, flipping through a fashion magazine that clearly had no connection to the case at hand. She wore a tight red V–neck shirt and black pants. Doyle occupied his usual spot on the couch. Angel leaned on the wall by the doorway to the inner office.

"In addition to what we already knew?" Cordelia replied. "Big fat zero."

"She's still in the grave, as far as I can tell," Doyle added. He ran a hand through his dark hair. "I didn't see anyone disturbin' her or visitin' her last night."

"I didn't get very far at the Rialto, either," Angel admitted. "All I found out is that we're not the only people suddenly interested in her."

"Maybe if she'd had this many people interested in her when she was alive, she'd still be here," Cordelia said.

"That's possible," Angel agreed. "Assuming everyone who's looking for her has her best interests at heart."

"That could be a big assumption to make," Doyle said. "And you know what happens when you assume. You make an—"

"Yes," Cordelia interrupted. "You start speaking in ridiculous and, may I say offensive, clichés."

"Point taken," Doyle said.

"Nothing new on-line, Cordy?" Angel asked, trying to steer the conversation back to the topic at hand.

"What could be new on a woman who died more than thirty years ago? It's not as if she was a celebrity or anything. Once she was in the ground, it looks like the world forgot all about her. It's kind of sad, really. The price of not having fame."

Not a unique condition, Angel thought, remembering how he'd felt the night before, when he wondered if he was leaving any kind of mark on the world. Although it was possible that it didn't become a problem for Betty McCoy until after she was dead.

"I don't know if fame is all it's cracked up to be either, Cord," Doyle pointed out. "People not only refuse to leave you alone after you're dead, but you gotta put up with 'em not leavin' you alone while you're alive, too."

"Who do you think I am, Greta Garbo? Maybe I don't want to be left alone, except by those people who call all the time to get me to switch my long distance."

Almost as if on cue, the phone on her desk rang. She looked at it as if it were a rattlesnake that might bite her. It rang again. She continued to look.

"Gonna answer it, Cordy?" Doyle asked her.

"Those people are getting more sophisticated all the time," Cordelia announced. "Now they can tell when you're talking about them."

"Might not be a long distance offer," Angel pointed out.

Cordelia gave a soft laugh. "Sure, maybe it's a client," she said. "Like that ever happens."

The phone continued to ring. Angel caught Cordelia's gaze, arched one of his brows, inclined his head gently toward the device.

"Oh, all right," Cordelia said. She lifted the receiver. "Angel Investigations." She was silent for a moment, then handed it to Angel. "It's for you. It's Cagney. Or is it Lacey? I always forget."

Angel took the handset from her. "Hello."

"Hi, Angel," Kate Lockley's voice said.

"Kate. What's up?"

"I just wanted to let you know there's a new P.I. in town who's an even bigger pain in the neck than you are," Kate said smartly.

"Let me guess. Is his name Mike Slade?"

"It sure is. You know him?"

"Never met the gentleman. But then, I don't

exactly go to the private eye conventions. If they have conventions."

"But you've heard of him," Kate said.

"Just last night, in fact," Angel admitted.

"Sounds like he had a busy night. Where'd you run across him?

"He visited a Hollywood dump called the Rialto Lounge. Knocked the bartender around. Slade was looking for a girl who worked there in the early sixties."

"That's the guy."

"What else do you know about him?" Angel asked her.

"For starters, we think he died in 1961."

"But he's new in town?"

"That's what makes it interesting. Also, he shot a police officer today, and we think he killed another one last night."

"Sounds like pretty antisocial behavior for a P.I.," Angel offered.

"Oh, like you're all social butterflies," Kate shot back. "Listen, Angel. I know you sometimes end up involved in some strange cases. If you come across this guy again, or any more information about him, I want to know about it immediately, if not sooner. Okay?"

"Sure thing, Kate. Got a description or anything?"

"I have a photo taken when he was alive, and an

Ident-a-kit picture based on witness statements from this morning. Same guy, both times. And he wears clothes that look like they came out of the Salvation Army, thirty years ago."

"Old-fashioned suit, big hat?" Angel asked.

"You have seen him?"

"No," Angel said quickly. "That's how the bartender described him."

Kate spoke slowly, as if she wasn't quite sure she believed him. "All right, Angel. I want this guy before he attacks any more of our officers. You will let me know if anything turns up, right?"

"I will, Kate."

She said good-bye, and Angel hung up the phone, lost in his thoughts. Cordelia watched him for a moment. "What?" she finally asked. "You look as if you swallowed something that wasn't what you expected it to be."

"I almost did," Angel said. "Remember I said there was someone else at the Rialto looking for Betty McCoy?"

"Sure," Doyle said. "It was only, like, two minutes ago."

"Well," Angel went on, "Kate is looking for the same guy. His name is Mike Slade. He's a private investigator. He's wanted for killing a cop. Oh, and he's been dead for almost four decades."

"Same guy?" Doyle asked, incredulous. "What are the chances of that?"

"You had a vision about Betty McCoy, sent by the Powers That Be, right?" Angel said. "That means that Betty McCoy is in some kind of trouble. But she's dead."

"Right," Doyle agreed.

"So automatically we can't rule out dead people as suspects, any more than we can rule them out as victims." He indicated himself with his thumb. "We're not all lying peacefully in our graves."

"You think this Slade guy's a vampire?" Cordelia asked. "Or is Betty McCoy one?"

"I'm not saying anybody's a vampire," Angel said. "But it's one possibility. We have to keep our minds open and work even harder to figure out what's going on. I don't know if this Mike Slade is dead or not, but he seems to be dangerous, either way."

"What's our next step?"

"We need to find out more about Betty McCoy," Angel said. "She must have left some trace behind when she died. Find it. What happened to her personal effects? Did she have any family or friends who might remember her? I'll try to find out more about our mystery killer while you guys dig deeper into Betty."

"Right, boss," Doyle agreed. "Digging here."

"Oh," Cordelia said, clapping a hand over her mouth. Doyle and Angel both turned to her. "Should he?"

Angel stared blankly at her. "Should he what?"

"Should Doyle dig up Betty McCoy?"

"Let's save that option," Angel said, "and hope it doesn't become necessary."

"No kiddin'," Doyle said quickly. "And even if it does become necessary we're still gonna think three or four times before we do that."

"Some people are so sensitive," Cordelia said. "You're not used to hanging out with the dead?"

"Hey, there's a big difference between spending time with a vampire and bein' around a bunch of corpses."

Angel ignored the exchange. "While you're finding out what you can about Betty McCoy, I'll be looking into this new player, Mike Slade."

"That can't be his real name," Doyle put in.

"Is it any worse than Francis Doyle?" Cordelia asked.

"It's way worse," Doyle shot back, sounding deeply offended.

"We don't know if Slade's his real name or not," Angel said. "We'll find out, though. This guy needs to be reined in."

"Then let's get reinin'," Doyle said. "What are we waitin' for?"

"I don't know about you, but I'm waiting for that guy with the big book to walk in and say, 'Betty McCoy, this is your life,' " Cordelia said.

"You'll have to be the ones to write that book," Angel told her. "Seems that Betty McCoy needs someone to put together her story."

"I like stories," Cordelia said. "I'm there. Let's go, Doyle."

"Go where?"

"We'll start with the library. See if we can turn up anything we couldn't find on-line."

"And there's no graveyard involved?" Doyle asked hopefully.

"No graveyard," Angel agreed. "At least until the sun goes down."

CHAPTER EIGHT

Mike Slade stood at a phone booth outside a corner grocery store and flipped through the telephone book chained to it. There were a few Wechslers in the book, but no Harold or Hal. Not even an *H*.

So the guy had an unlisted number. Not surprising for someone who was a city bigwig now. Most politicians and crooks kept their numbers out of the book, Slade knew. And that wasn't where the similarities ended.

In the old days he'd have phoned Charlie Wilson, a contact in the LAPD, and had him run down Wechsler's address. But if the past day had taught him anything, it was that nearly everything changed. Most people Slade had known back then seemed to be dead now. Even if Charlie was still alive, Slade figured he'd probably be living in a trailer somewhere, fishing and drawing Social Security, not still behind a desk in the Police Administration Building.

No, Slade had to assume he had no allies among the cops.

But that didn't mean he was without resources. He flipped to the front of the book and found an address for the Hollywood branch of the phone company. It wasn't far away, so he decided to hoof it. In person, he could get Wechsler's address out of them, he figured.

Anyway, detective work was all about legwork. An eye had to get face-to-face with the people he was talking to. It was too easy to lie over the phone when he had no way to see their faces, see if they were sweating out their answers or telling the truth.

Cabs were too expensive and hard to come by. People seemed to drive their own cars now, by themselves—mostly big truck-like vehicles that sat up high off the street. *Still, with as much traffic as there is these days, maybe that's the way to go,* he thought. *Make sure you can see and be seen.*

He shuddered, thinking about trying to drive in the kind of traffic that seemed to be everywhere these days. He used to love tooling up the coast with the car window down, feeling the wind in his face and smelling the salt air. But the streets in his day weren't as jammed as they were now.

One thing about being dead—there were lots of pleasures he would never have again. During the time he'd been truly dead, he didn't know or care. Now that he was back, he felt a deep sadness, fully aware of all the things he figured he would never experience again.

The phone company office, a big building made of stark gray stone, stood on a corner. It had double glass doors with metal pulls. The hours were posted on a sign fastened to one of the doors. It didn't look like a friendly place, but neither was it as formal and forbidding as City Hall.

And he couldn't see any of those doorways that led to nowhere and detected a gun inside one's coat.

He went in.

Inside was a big lobby, almost like a bank. There were windows like tellers' cages, with employees behind them. People were standing in lines, waiting their turn to get to a window and order phone service or complain about the service they had or perhaps cancel their service, if anyone could afford to be without a phone these days. With the difficulty of getting around and the high cost of pay phones, Slade thought it must be more important than ever to have your own telephone in your house or risk being cut off completely from the rest of the world.

He picked one of the lines at random and stood in it.

The woman in front of him clutched a phone. She looked like an immigrant from Europe. She was small and apple-cheeked, with a plaid scarf over her hair and a heavy coat on even though the day was warm. She carried the phone like a baby, as if it were a precious instrument.

He waited while she did her business and stepped away from the window, and then he approached. The woman behind the counter was a pretty young Latina named Luisa, according to the shingle on her window. He smiled at her.

"Hi, Luisa," he said. "My name's Slade. Mike Slade."

She smiled back. "Good afternoon, Mr. Slade," she said. "How can I help you today?"

He leaned in a little closer to her and slid a business card onto the counter. "I'm a private eye, see?"

"I see."

"Well, I'm looking to track down this jamoke. He's a bad egg. A killer, if you know what I mean."

"And how can I help?" she asked, her voice almost conspiratorial.

"He's got an unlisted number," Slade told her. "I don't care about that, I just need an address. I have to arrest him, make sure he does his time."

"Don't the police generally arrest people?"

"You know how they are; they won't move until they know they can get a conviction. And this guy's one of them, a fat cat. He's in with the mayor and his crowd."

"He's a politician?"

"That's right."

She laughed. "Maybe in other cities that would come as a surprise."

"So can you help me? His name's Wechsler. Harold Wechsler."

"I'm sorry, Mr. Slade," she said, glancing at his card. "I can't give out unlisted numbers. Or addresses."

"But you know what I mean, right? The cops are never going to bring him in. He's too powerful."

"Mr. Slade, there's nothing I can do for you. If you'll please step aside so I can help someone whom I can help."

"Just an address," Slade pleaded, his voice rising.

"Mr. Slade, if you'd like to speak with someone in management, I'm sure they can explain the same thing to you. If a party chooses to be unlisted, that means he is unlisted—to everybody."

"Luisa, this guy has killed people. He killed a gal I know, couldn't have been any older than you are."

"Then you should take the matter to the police. Please don't make me call Security."

"Hey, buddy, move it along," someone behind Slade said.

"Yeah," another voice agreed.

Slade turned. The people behind him in line were arrayed in a rank against him. Their faces held scowls, mouths downturned, foreheads lined.

"She told you she can't help you. Let someone else have a turn."

Slade reached inside his coat and pulled out the Browning. He showed it to the guy at the head of the line. "You just stay back," he said. "Luisa, I'm telling you, I want that address."

But Luisa didn't answer, and when Slade glanced back to look at her, she was gone.

Movement coming toward him caught his eye. Security guards in gray uniforms with black ties. And big guns in their hands.

Two of them. Angling for position.

"Drop that weapon!" one of them called.

Second time today I've heard that, Slade thought. He raised his .38 and fired a single shot.

A guard spun around and went down.

Slade ran.

Twenty minutes later Slade sat down on a bus stop bench, breathing hard. *This is getting old,* he thought. *Shooting and running. People get so upset when they see a piece these days.*

Someone had sure spoiled this town for private eyes.

In the old days, showing your gat was a good way to get a little respect and information, all at the same time. People took you more seriously if you carried one. And the private investigator's license made it legal to carry concealed.

Now the minute you pulled it, someone was there telling you to drop it.

Never surrender your weapon: that lesson had been burned into him during his brief tenure on the police force, and he had lived by it during his time as a private op. *Anyone tells you to drop your gun, they don't have your best interests at heart,* he thought. *Soon as it's on the ground they'll most likely start firing themselves.*

Slade only fired to wound. Unlike many of the private eyes he'd known, he had never killed a man. But he was a crack shot, and he knew when he pulled the trigger where the bullet would hit. His years in the grave hadn't dulled that talent a bit.

But even so, these people acted like he was killing right and left. As soon as he'd fired on that security guard—even though the guy had his own rod out and looked like he meant to use it—alarms had started to shriek. Slade had barely made it out of the area before sirens began to scream and black-and-whites came rolling in from every direction. After buying an obscenely expensive chocolate bar, he had ducked down an alley and in through the back door of a movie theater. Considering how much everything else now cost, he was afraid to see how expensive a movie ticket might be. The movie was already going on when he snuck in, and it was a bizarre piece of cinema. The camera work was jerky, the editing sloppy, with cuts every few seconds. Even the lighting was unnatural. There were more explosions than during the entire Korean conflict, he thought, and the patrons seemed to enjoy that, cheering one after another. Slade found the whole thing excruciating and slipped back out through the back door ten minutes later. He came out in the alley and hightailed it out of the neighborhood.

And he was still no closer to Wechsler.

But he had another idea.

He found a phone booth, looked up a number, and pumped thirty-five cents—part of the change from his candy bar—into the phone. When he got the tone, he dialed City Hall. He got an operator and asked for Harold Wechsler's office.

A few seconds later a young-sounding male voice answered: "Water and Power."

"Is this Harold Wechsler's office?" Slade asked.

"Yes, it is."

"Listen, don't disturb Mr. Wechsler if you can help it. I have a bit of a problem here."

"What is it?" the young man asked.

"I'm supposed to deliver this pool table that Mr. Wechsler ordered. He specifically asked for it to be there today—he's got a party coming up or something like that. Something about his new job, celebrating his appointment . . . I don't know."

"And the problem is?"

"The problem is I can't read the address they gave me at the shop. I can't tell if this says Benedict Canyon or Coldwater Canyon or Camino Real or what. It's all smudged, looks like someone was carrying it around in his pocket for a week."

"Can't you simply call your shop and ask whoever wrote it?"

"I could, but she went on her honeymoon yesterday. No one else there knows what the address was, and I can't even make out the letters clear enough to give them a hint. Look, I hate to bother him, but maybe you could just ask Mr. Wechsler. I don't want to get chewed out, but I don't want to lose my job, either."

"Hold on, I'll ask— No, wait, he's in a meeting."

"I can try again in a little while. It'll mean making some other deliveries first and working around his table. I put it in last because I knew he wanted it today for that party. You're probably going, huh? This table's a beaut. Try to get a game in."

"Perhaps it would be best if you did call back."

" 'Course if I end up across town, I might not get back in time, you know, what with traffic and all."

"Okay, fine. I'm sure it's not a problem," the young man said. "The street is Leona. It's near Coldwater, so maybe that's how you got confused."

"That could be," Slade said, hoping the relief in his voice sounded genuine. He knew Leona. It was short, winding back into the hills. "The number I got looks like 1711."

"No, no, it's 109," the young man said. "Perhaps you'd be best off if that person didn't come back from her honeymoon."

"Brother, you could be right," Slade said. "Thanks for your help. And enjoy this table."

He hung up.

Lucky break. If the kid had been invited to a party, he'd never have spilled.

But then, for him to have been invited, there'd have to have been a real party.

It was time for Mike Slade to get a car.

One thing Slade had found to be true of both Hollywood and Las Vegas: People had a tendency to run out of money in both places. That meant they sold those things that had value, such as cars. They sold them cheap because they weren't in a position to hold out for the best deal. And there were always other people with just enough money to buy them again, as long as they were still cheap.

Look for the neon lights, because that's where the cheap rides are.

Slade found the car he wanted at the second place he looked, a lot with the unlikely name of Reputable Motors. It was a marvel of Detroit engineering, a 1959 Plymouth Sport Fury convertible. There was enough chrome on its grille to plate a battleship, and its tail fins reached for the sky like a man with a gun pointed at him. It was pale yellow with a metallic gray stripe all the way down its side. If it was in factory condition, Slade knew there would be a 260 horsepower V-8 under the hood, with a four-barrel carb.

It was a sweeter ride than anything he had owned in life. He had once had his eye on a candy-apple red '58 Fury, but the '59 outclassed it in every possible way. The Sport Fury convertible had remained out of his price range.

But not anymore. He wandered onto the lot, looking at every other car, until a salesman came his way. There were some things that hadn't changed, and car dealers were one of those, it looked like. This guy wore a white shirt, with a dark tie, and blue slacks with dark checks. His hair was slicked back, and sweat beaded on his forehead right at the hairline. He smoothed his dark mustache with one finger as he approached Slade.

"See anything you like?" he asked.

"Lot of okay cars here," Slade replied, playing it cool. "Nothing special."

"I just want to let you know, every one of these cars has been thoroughly inspected by our mechanics. We have a hundred-point inspection we put every pre-owned vehicle through, so when we deliver it to you it's just like it was coming from the factory."

"That a fact?"

"That's right," the salesman said. He stuck out a hand. "My name's Daryl," he said. "Daryl Needham."

Mike clasped his hand, pumped it a couple of times. "Mike Slade."

"Well, Mike," Daryl continued, "I'd love to put

you behind the wheel of one of these fine machines."

"Maybe," Slade said, turning in a slow circle. "If I see anything that catches my eye."

"Let me ask you this," Daryl said. "Do you think if I could put you into a car you liked at a payment you could afford, that we could make a deal today?"

Slade scratched his chin as if thinking it over. "I think I could probably agree to that," he said.

"Well, that's the first step, then. You'd be amazed how many lookie-loos we get here on a daily basis. It's nice to spend some time with a man who knows what he wants and is prepared to do business. I guarantee you'll be glad you stopped in."

"I expect you're right about that," Slade said.

Hook baited. Time to reel him in.

Fifteen minutes later Slade was driving down the street behind the wheel of his dream car. Daryl had insisted on driving the car off the lot and then turning the wheel over to Slade once they had reached a stopping point. Daryl explained that it was the law, although he didn't seem clear on why it had to be that way. So they had stopped in front of a carpet store on Cahuenga, and Daryl came around to the passenger side, leaving the keys in the ignition. Slade slipped in behind the wheel.

"I think you're going to like driving this machine," Daryl said with an oily grin.

"I believe you're right," Slade told him. Then he

drew the Browning from beneath his coat and pointed it at the salesman. "Take a hike."

"Sir, you don't want to do this." His voice trembled a little with fear, but he kept that saleman's smile on just the same.

"What makes you think that? Get going."

"You're the boss," Daryl said, as agreeable as ever. He climbed out of the car and shut the door. Slade drove away, watching in his rearview as Daryl clenched his fists and glared after him. He turned a few corners, drove into another neighborhood, and then stopped long enough to figure out how to take the top down.

It was, after all, a glorious Los Angeles day.

Maybe that trip up the coast would happen after all.

CHAPTER NINE

Kate flipped the pages of the murder book on officer Deke Johannsen.

Every homicide case had a loose-leaf notebook assigned to it called a murder book. It quickly filled up with pieces of paper: witness statements, the coroner's report, the crime scene investigator's report, photos of any evidence found, and additional notes. Before long it would be full, and some homicides went into second and third notebooks. High-profile cases could reach a dozen, maybe more.

Kate had two murder books on her desk, Johannsen's and John Doe's. John Doe was the name given to the corpse found in private detective Mike Slade's closet. She was sure there was an intersection between the two cases, although at this point she didn't know what the common ground might be.

She was developing the beginnings of a theory, though, and she kept flipping through both murder books to see if anything caught her eye.

In her theory, the guy inside the closet was not Mike Slade. Slade had murdered someone in his office, hidden the body there (although why he would do that was still a huge question mark), and then vanished so he couldn't be tied to the murder. Now he had returned to kill some more, probably to hide some evidence that might have pointed to him. He had come to the demolition site at night, after the body was found, because something in that building could still implicate him after all these years. He had been discovered by officer Johannsen, and that discovery cost Johannsen his life.

Slade had to be in his seventies by now, which made the whole scenario a little more unlikely, she realized. But he was deranged, a murderer, haunted over the decades by his crime, and somehow still living in the sixties, when he had committed the murder that sent him over the edge. Now he believed he was still that age—he'd probably had plastic surgery, and he used hair dye to keep him looking more youthful. And he wore clothes from that period, as well. All the elements fell neatly into place.

If her theory was valid, then Slade was completely insane and wouldn't stop killing until he was captured or killed. He had left tracks across the decades, and now he would try to cover those tracks by killing everyone with whom he had ever been in contact. The girl he had been looking for at that bar Angel had mentioned—the Rialto?—was probably the next victim on his hit parade.

So Kate needed to look into missing person reports from late 1961. One of them would be the corpse. It would be male, and he would bear a strong resemblance to Mike Slade himself. The coroner had decided the body probably was Slade's, but that was without DNA evidence or dental records, just from his age, size, and a partial reconstruction of his face based on his skull. All guesswork.

And she needed to find people who had known Slade, because he'd be coming for them. If she could turn some up, maybe she could lay a trap.

She also needed to figure out how the attacks at City Hall and the phone company fit into things. At the phone company, according to the report that she had copied and placed in both murder books, Slade had been trying to get a phone number or address for a Harold Wechsler. He had claimed that Wechsler was a big-shot politician, so that had to be the new general manager of the DWP. He was old enough to have been around in Slade's heyday. He would be worth talking to.

Kate suddenly remembered something she'd seen in the John Doe murder book, that she hadn't really paid attention to before. She shoved the Johannsen book aside and opened the John Doe book to the witness statements. The most comprehensive of these was from a man named Blake, the foreman on the demolition project. He had called her the next morning and agreed to come in. He was interviewed for hours at Parker Center, where he was asked about every employee who had worked on the site and every person who had visited.

And one of those people, he recalled, was named Fetzer. No first name that he could remember. Fetzer had claimed to work for the head of the Department of Water and Power, and had demanded to be allowed into the building. Blake said that Fetzer couldn't provide any documentation that would permit him access, and demolition was already under way, so he had turned the man down.

Why does Fetzer want in? Kate wondered. *Does he really work for Wechsler? Does this have to do with why Slade wants to find Wechsler?*

Coming across the Wechsler connection from two different angles made it more than a random name. It was a clue, one of the first actual clues she'd turned up. She needed to check it out.

She stood, stretched, glanced at the clock on the wall. After seven. She had been at this all day, stuck inside the building, reading and making phone calls and writing notes and reading again. Her muscles were stiff; her neck and shoulders ached with tension. She massaged them for a moment as she stood there. Then she put the two murder books back into place on her desk, gathered her jacket and purse, and headed for the garage.

She needed to meet Fetzer, whoever he was, and Wechsler in person. This was potentially too important to do over the phone. She wanted to see their faces as they spoke.

Chances were slim that they'd be in the office this late on a weeknight. But it couldn't hurt to run by on the way home.

The parking garage was quiet, and Kate's footfalls sounded loud, echoing in the cavernous space. She usually parked far from the elevator, precisely so that on days like this one, when she got no exercise, at least she'd have to walk a few extra steps. She briefly considered stopping by the gym later on, but decided that would depend on how long she spent at City Hall and whether or not she tracked down Wechsler or his man Fetzer.

Some time on the StairMaster or spinning would sure help this tension, she thought.

She nearly jumped out of her skin when she heard the voice.

"Hi, Kate."

She let out a gasp of surprise. "Angel. You startled me."

He had appeared suddenly, standing next to her car,

even though she could have sworn she hadn't seen him there before. There were shadows at the front of the car, though, so he must have been hidden in them.

"Sorry."

"What are you doing here?"

"I wanted to talk to you," he replied.

"And I so love it when you startle me like that. So what is it you want to talk about?"

"This guy Slade. The P.I."

"You know any more than before?" she asked.

"No, but I think he ties into a case I'm working on. I was hoping you'd have a little more to go on."

She shook her head. "Angel, this is an open homicide case. And there's a dead police officer involved. You mustn't stick your nose into this."

Angel touched the end of his nose. "It's already there, Kate. I might be able to help. I just need to know what you have on him."

She looked around to make sure they weren't observed. "You want to go for a drive?"

"Thought you'd never ask."

He got into her car on the passenger side, and she took the wheel. She backed out of the space, exited the garage, and made a right turn. In a few minutes they were out on L.A. surface streets, driving randomly. She didn't want anyone to know that she had talked to Angel about this case.

"I'm serious about this, Angel," she began. "If you get in the way of this investigation, it's going to be bad news. The whole department is nervous about this case. Maybe not as nervous as I am, since I'm the one who caught it and at this point I'm the only one who knows how weird it is. But with one cop killed on duty and this guy Slade's visit to City Hall, by morning I expect the mayor to announce a task force and overtime and everything else to bring him in."

"I understand," Angel assured her. "I'll stay in the background. I am only interested in my case, but I think the two are tied together somehow."

"You going to tell me what your case is?" she asked, knowing he wouldn't. "Who's your client?"

Angel surprised her by smiling. "You wouldn't believe me if I told you."

"Anyone I know?"

"I'm sure not."

She made another random right turn, which put her onto Olympic. She could stay on this road all the way into Santa Monica and the Pacific Ocean, if she wanted to. But that wouldn't get her any closer to City Hall and Harold Wechsler. Instead, she pulled an illegal U-turn, taking Olympic back toward downtown.

"Okay," she said. "Here's what I've got. I'm really going out on a limb for you, Angel. I expect you to appreciate that, and I'm only doing it because I believe that if you come up with anything that will help bring this guy in, you'll share it."

"I will," Angel agreed.

"Good. Here it is, then. We have a corpse in Slade's old office building. Male, mid-thirties. We haven't been able to get a good I.D. on it. Coroner thinks it's Slade, but I'm not so sure."

"Because Slade seems to still be running around town?"

"Yes, that's part of it. Also, officer Deke Johannsen was murdered outside the same building last night. He was there to guard the building. I think Slade killed Johannsen to get into the building, to try to hide or remove evidence of the earlier homicide."

"Makes sense."

"Except that Slade must be in his seventies by now. People that age are rarely homicidal maniacs. But anything's possible, right?"

He was quiet for a moment, so she went on.

"Now here's something else—you've heard of Harold Wechsler?"

"Name's familiar, but I can't place it."

"He's the new general manager of the Department of Water and Power. Just took office last week, appointed by the mayor. Apparently one of his employees was at the building just before the body was discovered. And when Slade shot up a phone company office yesterday, he was looking for an address for Wechsler."

"So these two guys are looking for each other," Angel commented.

"Seems like it," Kate said. "I don't know yet what Wechsler wants with Slade. But based on Slade's track record, if he finds Wechsler, I imagine there'll be bullets involved." She paused. "Well, except for one thing. So far, we know he's done two shootings that have been witnessed. A police officer at City Hall, and a private security guard at the phone company. Both times, the victims have been wounded, but neither time were any slugs or shell casings recovered."

"That's odd, isn't it?"

"Yes," Kate agreed. "Very odd."

"So where are you headed now?" Angel asked.

"That's not for you to know," Kate told him. "Can I drop you someplace?"

"Anywhere," Angel said. "My car's back at your office, but I can catch a ride back."

"It's not that far out of the way," Kate offered. "Just don't ask me any more questions about this case. And don't forget what I told you about staying out of the way."

"Not a chance," Angel assured her. That response was sufficiently vague, he realized. Did he mean there was no chance that he'd stay out of the way, or no chance that he'd forget? He wasn't saying.

Kate dropped Angel off at his car, which was parked outside her building, and continued on to City Hall. She was troubled by his refusal to share any details of his case, but was accustomed to private investigators playing their cards close to the vest. They wanted to protect the privacy of their clients, and sometimes they were worried that if someone else solved their cases, they wouldn't get paid. Some investigators had their clients hire them through attorneys, because then all interaction was covered by attorney-client privilege. Kate at least trusted Angel to come clean if he learned something that would be helpful.

Inside the City Hall lobby, she showed her badge to the night guard, a heavyset black man with short salt-and-pepper hair. He looked at it, and when she asked for Wechsler, he had her wait while he dialed the office.

After a moment he put the phone down. "Sorry, detective," he said. "No answer. Voice mail's on. Looks like Mr. Wechsler is gone for the day."

"Can I just take a look?" she asked.

"No, ma'am. Nothing personal, but we're on alert here, since the incident. You know what I mean?"

"Yes, I understand."

"If there was someone up there to let you in, I could let you go up. But I can't let you go by yourself."

"Okay, thanks," Kate said, disappointed. She hadn't really expected anyone to be there, but she still felt thwarted.

On the way back to her car, another thought occurred to her, and instead of driving to the gym, she went back to her office.

If Slade has targeted Wechsler, she thought, *he might have found some other way to locate him. He could even have followed Wechsler home from City Hall.*

Time to put the city official under round-the-clock guard. If Slade was gunning for Wechsler, he'd be in for a surprise.

CHAPTER TEN

There were too many unexplained aspects to this case—if it was indeed a single case and not a series of unrelated coincidences—for Angel to completely accept Kate's theories. But she had given him more information than he'd had before, and putting it together with what little he knew about Betty McCoy, he was more convinced than ever that the whole thing was beyond the ability of the LAPD to deal with.

Kate was a good cop, but she was only human. She didn't really know what went on in the suprahuman world—and what they were facing here definitely had its roots in that realm.

He was back in the Belvedere GTX, racing toward Hollywood over surface streets. The streetlamps and neon of nighttime Los Angeles flashed by as he drove, watching for police cars and obeying

117

red lights, but anxiously, fingers drumming on the wheel as he waited.

Whatever was going on, it had to be wrapped up before more people died. With any luck, Angel could wrap it up before Kate had to face any tough questions about the nature of life and death. Angel felt oddly protective of her. At the same time, he wanted to keep the secrets of the night from being tugged into the light of day, and he knew that the death of a police officer, a crime that would not be allowed to go unavenged, could do just that.

Unless I figure it out first, he thought, *and offer up an explanation that will be accepted as rational by the human world.*

First stop, Argyle Avenue.

He parked two blocks away from the demolition site. He knew the police presence would be significant. They'd be watching the site from the ground and also probably from hiding, looking on from nearby apartments or hotel rooms and from the rooftops—in case the killer of Officer Johannsen returned.

Angel left the GTX at the curb and rounded a corner onto Argyle. A homeless woman slept curled under a thin blanket against the wall of a shoe store. At least that was what she looked like. Angel assumed she was an undercover cop and kept going, eyes on the ground as if he had no particular destination in mind.

At the next corner, still a block away from the

demolition site, he turned off Argyle, to the right. He figured he was being watched, so he'd throw the watchers off, let them believe he had no interest in the building. He went to the end of that block, made a left, crossed the street.

Now he was on the same block as the demolition site, but at the opposite end. On this side of the block were a smoke shop, an antiquarian bookstore, a plumbing supplies store, and a residence hotel. Angel picked the hotel.

Inside the front door, a desk clerk sat behind a window of bulletproof plastic, watching a tiny television. Sounds of battle from some miniature war wafted through the plastic, where angled slots served as a speaker. The clerk was involved in his program, or perhaps he was asleep. He didn't look up as Angel entered. Probably people came at all hours of the day and night anyway—it didn't look like a high-security kind of place to Angel. More like a place where people lived on their way down to the streets, or climbing back up from them. People who couldn't make the rent on a monthly apartment, but could scrape up the money for a week at a time, and continued to do so as weeks rolled into months and months into years.

Past the desk clerk there was a staircase and an elevator cage. The elevator looked as if it had been built in the twenties and last serviced at around the same time. Angel chose the stairs. They creaked as he climbed, but he doubted the desk clerk could hear over the fusillades erupting from his little television. The staircase smelled as if it hadn't been washed in fifty years or so, and Angel didn't even want to think about the sources of the odors.

The hotel was seven stories tall, but the stairs continued past the seventh floor, as Angel had anticipated they would. One more flight up was a padlocked door with the word "Roof" painted on it in faded black letters. Angel took the padlock in his hand and yanked down on it. The hasp tugged free from the old rotted wood. The door swung open. Angel stepped outside into the night.

There was a fresh breeze up here. Eight stories up, the wind seemed to gather its scents from the hills surrounding the city instead of from the city streets. Angel liked the rush of it against his cheeks, blowing away the close, stale air of the dingy stairwell.

He crossed the gravel-topped roof. The next roof was slightly lower, a jungle of air-conditioning units and ducts. Angel lowered himself over the side wall of the hotel, dropped to the adjacent roof, and worked his way around the ducts. Crossing that roof put him next to the roof of the demolition site.

The roof of that building was more or less intact. The demolition work had all been inside work— load-bearing and exterior walls and the roof would come down after the inside was gutted. Before crossing over to it, Angel went to the corner of the roof he was on, bent over the side wall, and looked down.

He could see one police car parked on Argyle in front of the building. He had seen it from the street, too, and knew there were two cops inside it. From down below, he had seen two other cops standing at the gate into the site. Now, looking down, he could see an open window in an apartment house across Argyle, with a camera mounted on a tripod aimed down toward the street. That was definitely police as well. Then there was the woman on the sidewalk, who he assumed to be an undercover officer. There were probably some more, scattered about inside the building. He couldn't see them from here.

He stood very still, listening. Human beings breathed, their hearts hammered in their chests, they moved and scratched and fidgeted. Angel could hear two of them, in the building below him. There could be more, others who were better able to keep still. But two, for sure.

At least he had a sense of the odds. Of how he had to move.

He had been one with the shadows for centuries. He stepped onto the roof of the Argyle Avenue building, and stopped. Soundlessly, he lowered himself to the roof's pebbled surface. He pressed his ear to it. No movement inside, other than the involuntary motions he'd already detected. He rose to a crouch and went to the roof-access hatchway. He expected it to be unlocked, and it was; the last thing a demolition crew wants is to be slowed down by having to negotiate locked passageways.

He opened the hatch and peered down into the darkness inside, lit only by light that strayed in from the street through broken windows and partially demolished walls. Sensing no movement, he started down the stairs.

Every few steps he stopped and listened again. As far as he could tell, the officers inside the building were on the ground floor, figuring that anyone who tried to come in would come that way. His soft footfalls on the stairs didn't seem to raise any alarm.

Reaching a landing, he paused, listened, then kept to the shadows as he circled around to the next flight of stairs. Slade's office, he remembered, had been on the fourth floor. Angel worked his way down to that level, moving slowly and silently.

A few minutes later he stood inside what had been Mike Slade's office. There was nothing left of the office but rubble, piles of brick and boards and dust. The closet in which the corpse had been found still stood, its door hanging open like a coffin lid. Angel stepped into the closet, into the space where Slade—or someone—had lain for so many years.

He smelled the air. The sweet, lingering scent of death. And something more. Hard to pin down. A tangy, electric smell that Angel always associated with the supernatural. With life after death.

Something had happened here, he knew. It wasn't just a dead body that was found. Something more than that.

He couldn't say just what. But he had some ideas.

"Freeze!"

The cop's Maglite blinded him. In the instant that it struck his eyes, he saw that the officer held a gun in one outstretched hand, a flashlight in the other.

The cop was as good at moving soundlessly as Angel was. Maybe better.

But there were some definite advantages to being a vampire. Two that came to mind were strength and speed. Angel didn't want to hurt a police officer, though, and neither did he want to spend the night in custody. There was too much at stake in tracking down Slade and stopping him before he could kill again. So he chose speed.

Before the cop could react, Angel threw himself to the floor, dropping beneath the beam from the flashlight. He rolled twice, directly toward the police officer, as the man scrambled to locate him again. Then Angel sprang to his feet, driving himself straight into the cop's solar plexus. He didn't slam into the man hard enough to hurt, just enough to knock the wind out of him and keep him from shouting. At the same time, he smacked the flashlight from the cop's hand. It sailed across the room, landing with a clatter in the dark.

Below him, Angel could hear the rest of the police officers beginning to respond to the sounds of fighting from above. Rays of light pierced the dark. Angel ran for the stairs and bounded back up to the roof.

The police gave chase. The sounds of pursuit were unmistakable now—voices raised in alarm, heavy footfalls on the stairs. But by the time the cops came up through the demolished building, Angel was on the roof of the building next door. By the time the police reached the roof, he was heading down the malodorous stairwell of the residence hotel.

He burst out into the lobby. The night clerk was staring into space, his expression blank, as if he'd fallen asleep with his eyes open. Angel gave him a small wave as he ran past. The guy began to sputter something after him, but Angel was already out the door and on the street.

The screams of sirens split the night, so he didn't go straight back to his car, but instead ran several blocks out of his way, then slowed to a casual saunter and approached his car from the far side of the Argyle Avenue building. Two police cars roared past him as he walked, but didn't give him a second look.

As he turned the key in the Plymouth Belvedere's ignition, Angel thought, *Well, that was a big waste of time.*

But he knew it wasn't.

He had learned nothing concrete about Mike Slade.

But he had come away with one unassailable fact: whoever had been dead inside Slade's closet wasn't dead anymore.

As he drove away from the area, he dialed a number on his cell phone.

"Angel Investigations," Cordelia Chase answered.

"Hi, Cordy," Angel said.

"Oh, it's you," she replied. "Having a nice evening? I hope you're enjoying your night on the town while we research drones stay inside and look at our computer screens twenty-four hours a day."

"It's great," Angel replied, refusing to be drawn in. "Anyway, Cord, I have a change of plans."

"Really?" she asked, enthusiasm brightening her voice.

"Yeah. Give up on Betty McCoy for now."

"That'll be easy, seeing as how there's absolutely no information on her in the world."

"That's okay. Move on to Mike Slade. See what you can find out about him."

"That's the dead private detective?"

"One and the same," Angel told her. "Same deal. He must have had some belongings, maybe more than Betty, because he had a business, paid taxes, the whole thing. He must have left more traces behind when he disappeared than Betty McCoy did. We need to find those traces, and see where they lead."

"So what you're really saying is, more computer work. I think my eyeballs are turning square from staring at that screen."

"Have Doyle do some of it."

"A funny thing about Doyle that maybe you haven't noticed. When he surfs the Web, all the sites that come up seem to have on-line betting or naked girls on them."

"Maybe you should do it," Angel agreed.

"That's what I'm thinking. Maybe there's some kind of rent-a-geek service. Should I look in the phone book?"

"Cordelia . . ."

"I'll do it," she moaned.

"In the morning you can hit the city records office," Angel suggested.

"I'll be staying up all night on-line," Cordelia complained. "You expect me to be awake in the morning too?"

"We all make sacrifices," Angel assured her. "One more thing."

"Oh, of course, because I'm not even close to busy enough already."

Angel ignored her tone. "I need an address for Harold Wechsler. This is urgent, so find it and call me back as soon as you can."

"Yes, sir," Cordelia said. "Anything you say, sir."

Angel thanked her and disconnected. He put the phone away and kept driving, with no destination in mind. Angel was afraid Slade would keep going after Wechsler, so until the dead P.I. was found, that was what he needed to do as well.

As he cruised through the dark L.A. night, he turned the case over and over in his mind.

That got him exactly nowhere.

CHAPTER ELEVEN

Harold Wechsler lived on Leona Street, off Benedict Canyon. The address suggested wealth and prestige. Those two attributes were things that Wechsler had spent his adult life striving for, but they were really incidental to his real goal. Wealth and prestige could help him achieve that goal, however, so that made them desirable.

The real goal was power. Rich, famous people tended to have better access to power than poor nonentities. So Wechsler saw those attributes as necessary stepping-stones to where he was really going.

The journey had been a long one. But it was almost done. The destination was within reach.

He sat in his expansive living room, enjoying the plush furniture, the thick off-white carpet. His home theater system filled one end of the big room. It had cost him twenty thousand dollars to buy and install, and he had paid cash for it. He knew that was a lot of money to some people, and he took great joy in being able to spend it on a whim. He had once spent sixty thousand on a single party that lasted three hours.

The most cash he had ever spent had been eleven years ago. He had delivered it in a suitcase, a big green Samsonite, to the conference room of a downtown law firm: $125,000.

What he bought with it was a man's life. Or, more specifically, his death.

Wechsler had no regrets about that. The man had been in his way. Thwarting his ambition. Then the man was dead, and one more roadblock was out of his way. Most murders were considerably less expensive, but one paid the price to get the job done, and this particular victim was worth double the one and a quarter he'd paid.

Now that his ultimate goal was almost within his grasp, though, there was another possible roadblock. Whatever the cost, this one needed to be cleared away too.

He turned to the three men sitting together on a butter-soft brown leather sofa. Barry Fetzer, Ryan Laine, and Luis Reyes. These three trusted lieutenants had been with him since the early days. They knew—figuratively and literally—where the bodies were buried.

They'd planted several of them.

They had been kids when Wechsler started his climb—he'd barely been in his twenties, himself. Starting small, a two-bit punk trying to make a name for himself in the big city. Los Angeles was where people came to reinvent themselves, where who one was yesterday didn't matter as long as one had an act, some good patter, and the illusion of success.

Hal Wechsler had moved here from Kansas City, where the mobs were well entrenched, inbred. Where the only way up was through the ranks, and everyone already knew who would be the next boss, and the one after that.

That was no good to Wechsler. He didn't want limitations put on his progress by other people. So he went west, not stopping until the ocean washed up over his feet, ruining a pair of good Italian shoes.

They'd been expensive. It didn't matter. He'd be able to afford more.

In L.A. there were gangs, but there were a lot more newcomers. Things were less established, less settled. Wechsler was able to carve out a piece of territory for himself.

And then he fell in with some interesting people. The kind he'd never heard of in K.C. Sometimes they wore dark hooded robes and burned candles and incense and chanted what sounded like nonsense.

But sometimes they got results.

And they were willing to teach.

Wechsler immediately saw the possibility of combining his two hobbies. L.A.'s underworld had not been exposed, in those days, to the world of magic.

As soon as Wechsler put them together, he began his rise to the top. It wasn't too many years before he had a respectable name in the city. He traded on that, building alliances, cultivating the right friendships.

These men—Fetzer, Laine, Reyes—had been dragged up with him. They were all worth more than they'd ever had a right to hope for. Wechsler fingered his silk robe, enjoying the way it slid between his fingers, and then spun on them.

"You blew it!" he shouted by way of opening. He was looking straight at Fetzer.

"We've been over this, boss," Fetzer protested. "They wouldn't—"

"I know. I'm tired of hearing about it."

"So what do you want?"

Wechsler held out his hands as if he couldn't believe what he was hearing. "What do I want? I want Slade. You were supposed to perform the binding spell before they released him. You didn't, so he's out. And he's after me, by all reports. I don't know if he can really interfere with my plans, but I don't want to take that chance."

"How are we supposed to find him?" Reyes asked. "We're surrounded by cops now."

"Whose fault is that?" Wechsler asked angrily.

"My only concern is that you do find him. Before he finds me. Is that understood?"

"Got it," Ryan Laine promised.

"So why are you sitting there?" Wechsler demanded. He waved his hands at Laine and Reyes. "You're just taking up space. Get out there. Use reinforcements if you have to, but find Slade!" They all knew what reinforcements meant. Demons. Wechsler had a number of them in his employ. He didn't like to use them for anything requiring diplomacy or sophistication, but when he just needed muscle there was nothing better.

Laine and Reyes got off the couch as one and headed for the door. Before they were through it, Wechsler turned to Barry Fetzer. "You're in charge of this," he hissed. "If they fail, it's on you."

"Got it, Hal," Fetzer assured him, nodding.

"See that you keep it in mind."

Angel stood in the tall grass that covered the hillside rising up behind Wechsler's house. At least a half-dozen police cars were parked in front—so many cops standing on the dark roadway that it looked like a parade route. Angel had driven casually past them and parked a couple of miles away. He had jogged back, circled around a neighbor's house, and come out behind Wechsler's, where he had an eagle's-eye view of the property. It was a lovely house, white stucco, very modern, with large expanses of glass facing the hills.

There were many lights on inside, despite the hour. In one room, Angel could see four men talking—arguing, it looked like. *Maybe Wechsler's an insomniac,* he thought. *Maybe these are his poker buddies.*

Or maybe something is going on.

Angel decided he needed a closer look.

He started to inspect the lay of the land, to see if there was a safe way to get nearer without being spotted through those big windows. A hundred yards below his position, floodlights bathed the hillside and the wide lawn that led up to a flagstone patio surrounding a brilliant blue pool, illuminated from within. Here Angel was safe in the dark, but when he started to move in he'd have to traverse a well-lit swath of grass.

As he watched, a movement of grass down below caught his eye. *Animals? Birds? Or something else?*

He watched the spot carefully, half expecting to see a coyote emerge from the thick growth.

Instead, a hat appeared. In the dark, it looked like a gray fedora. Beneath it, a big head, then broad shoulders in a gray suit coat.

Mike Slade!

The private eye was farther down on the hillside, closer to where the bright lights washed the grassy slope and the neatly trimmed lawn. And he was moving nearer, his sights set on the house.

In his hand, as he moved out of the high grass, Angel saw a gun.

Slade was making his move. So Angel made his.

He transformed himself, feeling the rush of power that coursed through him as his features were altered. In this state, Angel couldn't pass for human, but in this state, the urgency of doing so seemed faraway and without import. Sometimes the vampire bit helped by distracting or surprising his opponents, so it was a card he played when he thought it might work.

With a low, guttural snarl, Angel charged down the hillside. Thick grass clutched at his legs but he pushed through it with his powerful strides. It rustled as he ran, though, and his quarry heard the noise.

Slade turned, a look of amazement on his face—but not fear, Angel noted—and pointed his gun up the slope. He squeezed the trigger three times.

Angel threw himself down into the grass as soon as Slade took aim. He heard bullets whistle through the tall grass just over his head; then heard the reports, three loud cracks, that traveled up the hill more slowly than the slugs themselves.

"Show yourself, demon!" Slade called. "Make your play! You ain't got a chance!"

Demon?

How many people would automatically assume that Angel was a demon? *Only those who had some experience with the matter,* Angel thought. Of course, there was no telling what Slade might have learned while he was dead.

Or what he had learned while he was alive that resulted in his being killed.

Curiouser and curiouser, Angel thought.

He worked his way through the grass, staying low, trying not to let the rustling reveal his position to Slade. Bullets wouldn't kill Angel. Normal bullets, anyway. But he didn't know what Slade was firing. If the man had indeed returned from the grave—and brought his gun with him—who knew if the gun fired real bullets. Perhaps the whole thing was some supernatural construct that shot phantom bullets. That could explain the fact that no slugs or shell casings had been found at his shooting scenes.

And there was no guarantee that a supernaturally powered weapon wouldn't hurt Angel.

He wished he could see Slade. He figured Slade was probably wishing he could see Angel. Slade's position, Angel knew, was perilous—his shots would have alerted the police and the household, and he was trapped between them and Angel.

Angel heard another sharp crack, and a slug tore into the grass directly in front of him. He threw himself backward and sideways, dropping out of sight into the grass again.

From the direction of the house, Angel could hear raised voices.

Lots of them.

Unless Slade was crazy—crazier than Angel already suspected—he wouldn't run toward the voices. He'd run away from them.

He'd be headed right toward Angel.

Angel pushed himself up on his hands and feet, weight resting on the balls of his feet, muscles tensed, ready to spring as soon as Slade came near. He was coiled like a sprinter at the starting blocks.

As the voices came closer, Angel could hear a rustling through the grass. Raising his head slightly over the tall grass, he saw Slade heading his way, backing up the hill away from the searching police. They were using bright flashlights now, sweeping the beams this way and that over the slopes. Slade was silhouetted between the house, the crazily shifting beams of flashlights, and Angel.

Angel waited.

Three more steps, up the hill. Walking backward, Slade stumbled once.

While he was off-balance, Angel lunged.

He slammed shoulder-first into Slade's midsection. Slade didn't feel dead. He felt solid and muscular. He let out a grunt when Angel plowed into him, and then his knees went out from under him.

Angel's momentum carried them both down the hill. Slade hit the ground first, and Angel sailed over him, keeping a grip on the detective's jacket. He curled up as he went, landing on his back, then pulled Slade down with him. Slade landed on Angel and bounced off, tumbling farther downhill. His jacket ripped, and Angel was left flat on his back with a piece of fabric in his hands.

He rolled over to see Slade pinned down by a dozen flashlight beams.

"There he is!" someone shouted.

"Freeze!" another voice called.

"I'd do it if I were you," Angel suggested.

But Slade gave no indication that he was ready to cooperate. He raised his gun and squeezed off two shots toward the police. Both shots found their mark and two officers went down.

The cops returned fire.

A hail of bullets flew up the hill. Angel pressed himself flat against the earth. Over his head, a dozen slugs whistled through the air, like mosquitoes buzzing past.

Except that these mosquitoes were hot lead, and they did more than sting.

The vampire knew the bullets wouldn't kill him. But they would hurt, and they'd slow him down, maybe long enough to prevent him from taking out Mike Slade before he could injure or kill another cop.

Of course, trapped here under a blizzard of bullets, he wasn't doing much good anyway.

Slade got off a couple more shots. Angel could distinguish his shots from those of the police, because Slade's reports were so much louder. Angel risked a glance. The cops had taken cover around Wechsler's house: behind columns, a big stone barbecue grill, a low adobe wall that ran between the pool and the lawn.

But Slade still stood there, dark against the white of the well-lit house, gun in his hand.

"Give it up, Slade," Angel hissed.

Slade spun around. His gun came with him.

"Who are you?"

"I just want to help," Angel said. "I don't want to see anyone get hurt."

"It's a little late for that, pal," Slade said. "There's plenty hurt already, see, and more that're gonna be hurt if I don't get to Wechsler."

"Look, this is no time to talk," Angel insisted. "Just drop the gun and surrender to me. I've got some friends on the force. We can take care of this."

"No deal, demon. Nothing to be taken care of," Slade replied. "I know I've bought myself a big world of trouble, shootin' at those flatfoots. But Wechsler—"

Again with the "demon," Angel thought.

"You're not going to get to Wechsler, so give it up," he said. "You can see how well he's guarded."

"If I don't get him tonight," Slade shot back, "there's always tomorrow."

"If you get out of here alive."

"I'm not too worried about that, tell you the

truth," Slade said. There was something in his voice that Angel couldn't quite identify. Regret?

"Then we have something in common," Angel told him. "Come on, just put down the gun."

"Not on your life, Mac."

He pointed the gun at Angel and pulled the trigger. Angel tried to dodge the shot, but it caught him in the shoulder, and he went down.

Another volley of bullets from the police down the hill flew up. Dirt kicked into Angel's eyes, and he shut them, clapping a hand over his shoulder against the fiery pain there.

With his eyes closed, he could only hear Slade rustling past, farther up the hill, away from his prey.

He didn't dare get up while the lead was flying.

When there was a moment of quiet, Angel rose to his knees, looking up the hill after Slade. There was no trace of the man. He was gone, into the dark hills and canyons. Angel could hear distant helicopters coming toward them, so maybe the police would be able to trap him in the hills.

Which left him. He needed to get out of there.

He gained his footing, unsteadily, one hand still holding his shoulder. The wound was already beginning to heal, but it still hurt. There was no exit wound, but somehow Angel sensed that there was no bullet left inside him.

He started to look for a way off the hillside when

139

a helicopter swooped by overhead, its powerful searchlight picking him out.

It flew past, then came around again, but the light operator kept the beam trained on him. Police came up the hill, shotguns and pistols in hand.

A voice boomed from the chopper. "Don't move. You're surrounded. Put your hands on top of your head."

Surrounded? Not by any definition I know, Angel thought.

Except maybe the one that counted. They weren't on every side of him, but they had him outnumbered and outgunned.

Of course, they had the wrong man.

But they didn't know that.

Angel put his hands on his head, let his face regain its human aspect, and waited for them. In a few moments the first officers reached him. One of them, a tall man with a thick red mustache and a spattering of freckles across his small nose, gave him a smile that was anything but friendly.

"You're under arrest, partner," he said. "Hands behind your back."

This is just what I needed, Angel thought. He did as he was told. The redhead snapped handcuffs around his wrists.

When more of the officers reached them, they walked him down the hill. He didn't say anything; he knew they wouldn't listen. Not here. Not with at least one of their own on the way to the hospital, or worse.

"You have the right to remain silent," the redhead began, reading Angel's Miranda rights off a small card he carried in his uniform pocket.

Angel decided to exercise that right.

CHAPTER TWELVE

Doyle couldn't figure out why this place creeped him out so.

Sure, it was full of dead people. That was what cemeteries were all about. Monuments to the dead, by which the living could remember those they'd lost.

But he'd been in cemeteries before, and while they weren't his ideal vacation spots, he could not remember one that gave him quite the willies that this one did. He was waiting for something to happen. He didn't know exactly what, but he figured he'd know it when it did.

In the meantime, he wandered among the shadowed rows of headstones, trying to keep a low profile in case whatever was going to happen came from on top of the earth instead of underneath it. He had his leather jacket buttoned against the night's chill, and he had his hands jammed in its pockets. A gibbous moon hung low over the cemetery walls, throwing shadows of the trees that lined the park and gave shade on hot days.

To pass the time, he started to look at the names and dates on some of the stones. The first time he'd been here he'd been so focused on watching Betty McCoy's grave that he had barely taken his eyes off it. But now he was resigned to the fact that nothing was going to happen there, so he roamed the rows of headstones. Chester Morgan, 1976. Henry Fitts, 1924. Suzannah Burstrom, 1958. Harris Stetko, 1999.

As he meandered up and down the rows, he noticed that some names seemed to be repeated. The first ones he noticed were the Villareals. Then there were the Doans. Clusters of them. There were several Morgans, a few Riddles here, a clutch of Stetkos there. The more he noticed the repeating names, the more the fine hairs on the back of his neck began to stand up.

Because he realized that he recognized some of the names on the stones.

The Villareals and the Doans and the Riddles. It took Doyle a few minutes to place them, but then he realized that they were not the names of humans he'd known.

They were the names of demons.

Demons lived among the human population with

varying degrees of success. Some passed quite well. Doyle himself had gone so far as to marry a human woman. The marriage hadn't lasted long, but he occasionally regretted the loss of it. Others kept to the shadows, the sewers, the back alleys, and didn't interact with humans at all unless it was to rip their heads off and eat their brains.

But these groups, the Doans and Riddles and Villareals, as well as the Barnetts and the Chongs, whose names he began to see now, were all families of demons that had passed as human. If it had just been one or two familiar names, he would never have put it together. But all of these, gathered here in one place . . . this was a burial ground for demons. Sure, some humans were mixed in, but Doyle had never in his life seen this many demons buried in one place.

No wonder it's creepin' me out, he thought. *It's kinda like a family reunion, only it ain't my family and none of 'em are alive to reunite.*

He remembered a party he'd been to once, at the Morgans' house. The Morgans were Mogranth demons, he remembered. Their natural appearance was red-skinned and many tentacled, but, like Doyle, they could mask that and appear completely human, at will. This particular branch of the family had held a party when they bought a new house in a suburban neighborhood, and invited the neighbors over. They ended up with more than a hundred people and demons in the house and yard.

As the party roared on into the night, the decibel level grew and grew. Finally, another neighbor, a couple of blocks over, called the police. They came and broke up the gathering.

But one of the younger Morgans, on hearing sirens and seeing the flashing lights and the armed officers gathering out in front, panicked and dropped his protective guise. One of the guests saw him and screamed.

The elder Morgans were able to convince the partygoer that too much alcohol had been consumed, and that Halloween preparations were under way, even though it was only mid-July. But the Morgans were chagrined that their cover had almost been blown so easily and so soon after buying the new house. They waited a year, then sold it and relocated to yet another quiet suburban neighborhood.

They never threw another party.

Doyle thought he heard a noise behind him and spun around, but it was just two branches rustling in the gentle breeze. *I'm jumpin' outta my skin*, he thought. *Gotta get a grip*.

He jammed his hands deeper into his jacket pockets and headed back over to where Betty McCoy's grave was. As far as he knew, she was human.

And he couldn't say why, but he found that some-how comforting.

There's something to this computer stuff after all, Cordelia thought. She had been at it most of the night, but she was beginning to find some satisfaction in the way one piece of information led to another and then another. *It's like putting together a jigsaw puzzle,* she thought. *You can't get one piece until you've got the ones around it, but once you do that, it all fits together like it was meant to be.*

And has my life really become so pathetic that this in any way resembles fun? she wondered.

She had switched from searching for information about Betty McCoy to looking up Mike Slade, the private investigator Angel had told her to track down. He had gone missing in the early sixties, but he, unlike Betty, had been somewhat of a Holly-wood fixture. There were several news stories about him, most of them trumpeting his solving of a few high-profile cases involving midlevel celebrities. It was interesting to read how he helped out starlets in distress and brought down drug dealers selling dope on studio lots. But it didn't really get her anywhere.

So she tried something she had heard Willow talking about, back when she lived in Sunnydale: public records.

For most law-abiding citizens, there are huge vol-umes of information in the public record. Births, deaths, marriages, beginnings and endings of businesses, Social Security numbers, passport applications . . . the list went on and on.

Of course, the public record didn't mean just anyone could go in and look at it. But Willow knew a few tricks to get access, and Cordelia found that she had picked up some of them. Her joy when she brought up the Los Angeles County tax rolls for 1961 surprised her.

Slade had just kind of disappeared in 1961. No death certificate had been issued, but the records relating to him came to an abrupt stop.

Prior to that, he had run his private investigation business on the books, so there were tax records. He hadn't made a lot of money, but he had done okay. And he had paid taxes for a full-time employee, whose Social Security number was listed.

So out of the county records, and into the federal ones. Cordelia found out that the Social Security number belonged to someone named Veronica Chatsworth.

Now she had a new name to trace. If Chatsworth had outlived her employer, she might know something about Betty McCoy. Cordelia started over, finding out everything she could about this new person.

After digging around in the databases for another couple of hours—and downing a cup of coffee to keep her eyes open into the wee hours—she learned that Veronica had been born in 1936 in Indianola, Iowa. She'd graduated from high school there and had worked for a drive-in restaurant before getting on a bus one day and riding for three days and two nights to Los Angeles. She had been in the city only briefly before being employed by Slade. She had remained in his employ from 1955 until 1961.

Following that, she had held a number of other jobs. In 1967 she had married someone named Vic Morris. Cordelia jotted that name down to look into when she had finished finding out what she could about Veronica Chatsworth. In 1977 she had given birth to a daughter named Barbara Morris. In 1990 she died of lung cancer.

Cordelia stood up from the desk and stretched. She'd been sitting for so long that she felt as if her bones were compressing. She walked around the office a couple of times, poured herself a cup of water from the freestanding cooler. Her footsteps were loud in the deserted office; the sounds of the early morning city seemed soft and distant. She could remember a time when staying up all night was fun—dancing, partying, letting the world pass by with no cares or responsibilities. Here in the dead hours of morning, that time seemed far away indeed.

Lacing her fingers together, she extended them as far as she could, and returned to the computer.

The names Vic Morris and Barbara Morris were scrawled on a notepad next to her keyboard, so she dug into Vic's life first. She only really cared about him as far as he intersected with Veronica Chatsworth. She learned that he'd been a police officer and that he had died in the mid-1990s. So she turned her attention to Barbara Morris, who, it turned out, was still alive, paying taxes, and attending the Los Angeles Police Academy.

Bingo.

A walking, talking connection—several times removed, but better than nothing—to Mike Slade and Betty McCoy.

Whether her parents had ever told Barbara Morris anything about the old days was, of course, the million-dollar question.

She found a phone number—*people would be appalled, really, to learn how much information about them is available on-line*, she thought—and dialed.

"Never heard of him," a groggy-sounding Barbara Morris said after a few moments of preliminary, sorry-I-woke-you-but-this-is-important conversation.

"Is that your final answer?" Cordelia asked.

"Yes. Now if you don't mind—"

"But your mother worked for him for years," Cordelia persisted. "Could she have saved any of his old case files, maybe in a garage or attic or someplace?"

"I'm really sorry, but I can't help you. I am not aware of any files, and I've never heard of this person you're asking about. Please don't call me again."

Cordelia heard a click and then a dial tone. She'd been hung up on. She hated that—if there was any hanging up on to be done, she liked to be the one to do it.

Barbara Morris would be no help. Maybe if she wasn't a cop-in-training, she wouldn't be so suspicious and hesitant. Of course, Cordelia had probably roused the woman out of a sound sleep to ask her about someone who had died long before she was born. Maybe being unwilling to talk about him was a reasonable response.

But it was also a response that left Cordelia at a dead end. She could, she supposed, go to bed. There were many compelling reasons to do that, not least of which was that she was finding it increasingly hard to keep her eyes focused. Sleeping wouldn't help in the long run, though. When Angel came home and wanted to know what she'd learned, he wouldn't be happy to hear that she had gone only so far and then given up. So she got out the Yellow Pages and riffled through them, hoping some new plan of action would come to mind.

And it did. She knew there must be files. The man ran a business; he paid taxes; he had to have kept files on his cases. Those files could have been taken to the city dump after his disappearance, but that seemed unlikely. The information contained in them would have been considered confidential, for one thing. If this Veronica Chatsworth had been any kind of employee she wouldn't have wanted the clients' personal lives scattered for the seagulls and dump scavengers to collect. And if she thought that Slade might come back from wherever he'd disappeared to, she would have wanted to keep the files around. If not in her home, then somewhere else.

She flipped to "Storage" in the Yellow Pages. And started dialing numbers.

By the time she reached "Valley U-STOR, Open 24 Hours," she thought her fingers were going to fall off from hours of punching the keyboard and then the telephone dial pad.

"Valley U-STOR," a male voice answered. Disturbingly peppy, considering the hour.

Cordelia put on her best sultry voice. "Good morning," she breathed. "My name is Cordelia, and I'm trying to locate some items that were stored in the early sixties. Were you open that long ago?"

"Well, I wasn't born that long ago," the man said. "But the business was here, sure. Been here since the Second World War, I think."

"So you're the manager?" Cordelia asked.

"Me? No, I'm just the guy who gets to work graveyard."

"That sounds like a very important job. What's your name?"

"I'm Doug."

"Hello, Doug. You can call me Cordy."

"Hi, Cordy."

"So do your records go back that far?"

"We're totally computerized now," he said, pride creeping into his voice. "If you stored something here in 1950 and you wanted to know what date you first rented the space, I could tell you."

"That's very impressive," Cordelia told him.

"Yeah. The owner, he's a pretty good guy. Smart. Likes to take care of the customers."

"That's great," Cordelia said. She'd already had similar conversations several times in the last hour and she wasn't holding out much hope for this one, but she had to try. "So if I gave you a name, you could tell me if that person stored some belongings there in 1961 or '62."

"I could, sure. The boss wouldn't want me to, though. Isn't that kind of a violation of privacy?" Doug sounded unsure of himself.

"Not really," Cordelia assured him. "I wouldn't be asking what was stored or trying to get access to it, just if there was something in a particular year. I know it's a management-level decision, but you sound like a decisive kind of guy."

"Well, I guess that'd be okay."

"Oh, good. The name is Veronica Chatsworth. Like I said, I don't know if it was in '61 or '62, but one or the other, probably 1962."

"Chatsworth? Hang on a sec."

She could hear him clicking keys on a keyboard. "It's checking," he said.

"I'm waiting," she said, playing him. "Do you work out? Your voice sounds so muscular."

"I play some hoops, surf, you know."

"I knew it." She smiled. He'd tell her whatever she needed to know.

"Here we go," he said. "Chatsworth, Veronica. Stored June 18, 1962. Billed now to a B. Morris in Silver Lake."

Barbara Morris. That liar!

"Thanks, Doug," she said. "How late do you work?"

"I'm on until eight," he said.

"I hope I get to see you soon."

"Uh, cool," he replied. She said good-bye, and hung up.

Was there anything worse than the Valley in the middle of the night? She thought about it for a moment. Outside of the Valley in the daytime, nothing came to mind. But it didn't matter. She was on to something now, and she needed to see it out as far as it would go. Besides, the drive would get her away from the computer and the phone, and that was a good thing.

ANGEL

As tired as she was of dialing, she tried one more number. But either Angel's cell phone was turned off or the battery was dead. He had lived for two hundred and forty-odd years, yet he was constantly defeated by a simple piece of technology.

She headed for her car.

CHAPTER THIRTEEN

Mike Slade screeched to a halt in front of Barbara's Silver Lake house and climbed out of the Fury. The city was getting too hot. He needed a place to lie low while he came up with another way to get to Wechsler. The guy had an army of cops around him, and he was in good with the mayor, so the word of one long-dead private eye wasn't going to be good enough to put him away. Slade needed to come up with some solid proof that the joker was a wrong guy.

And through Barbara, he had an insider on the police force.

In his day, cops had been the natural enemies of P.I.'s. L.A.'s finest had been known far and wide for being as dirty as they came. They brutalized, they extorted, they ran numbers for gangsters like Mickey Cohen. They hated private eyes, because private eyes weren't important enough to be on the take, so their interests could come into conflict at any time. And if the cops ever did their job, that would be one less case that would end up in the lap of a P.I.

So every private dick that Slade knew was friendly with one or two cops, because every now and then they had to be pumped for information. But P.I.'s avoided the rest of the force like the plague.

He had some sense that things were different now. For one thing, they allowed women on the force. And he couldn't see any daughter of Veronica being dirty, even if her dad had been a cop. He figured he had to trust her.

Anyway, he had no one else to go to. Everyone he'd known seemed to be dead. His only connections to his own time were Barbara Morris and Hal Wechsler. One of them he wanted to take care of, and one he wanted to see dead.

He knew it was late, and he regretted doing it, but he pounded on her door.

After a couple of minutes she opened it. Her service revolver was in her hand again. Her brown hair was mussed, and her eyes were slits.

"Oh, it's you. The friendly ghost detective."

"Can I come in, Barbara?"

"If I said no, you'd probably just turn into mist and drift through the door or something, wouldn't you?" Her voice was thick with sleep.

"I don't know if I can do stuff like that," he replied. "I don't think I'm so much a ghost as . . . well, I don't know what to call it." He suddenly remembered the demon he had seen on the hillside behind Wechsler's house—maybe someone like that could do the mist trick. He squeezed his own arm. "Feels pretty solid to me."

"Come on in," she said. "Just don't expect me to be entertaining. Or conscious."

He followed her inside, locked the door behind himself. "Sorry to wake you," he said.

"You haven't," she assured him. "I took a sleeping pill earlier. I only look as if I'm standing up. I'm really sound asleep in bed."

"A sleeping pill? What's the matter?"

"I'm under a lot of stress," she explained. "Trying to get decent grades at the Academy and pay the bills and everything. Some nights I can't sleep so well. But I still have to function the next day. So I need a little chemical assist."

"Your doctor prescribes the pills for you?"

"No, Mike. They're an over-the-counter product. No prescription needed. But obviously they affect my thinking or I wouldn't even be telling you all this."

He shook his head. Amazing new world.

He found himself feeling very solicitous of Barbara, concerned about her. He was a different person in her presence, somehow. In the old days, he'd have been more direct with her, more profane. In a strange way, he felt like a father to her. He supposed it was because he had known her mother so well.

Loved her mother.

The thought stole unbidden into his mind, and he tried to push it away. But it was too late; like being told not to think about a green elephant, suddenly it was all he *could* think about.

And he figured there was truth to it.

Veronica had been just a kid, just an employee, at first. She was young, but she was smart and efficient, and she had organized his business affairs in no time. And she'd been a knockout. He could still remember her in a tight sweater and an equally tight skirt, bending over the bottom file drawer to put something away. They'd started having lunch together and talking during the day, and he'd been impressed by her thoughts and hopes and dreams. Then lunches had turned into dinners, and dinners into dates, movies, nightclubs, drinks.

Before he knew it, he was hopelessly smitten with his secretary. She seemed to return the feeling. He couldn't remember how many wonderful nights he'd passed in this very house, falling asleep next to her in her bed, waking up with her in his arms, warm and soft and comfortable.

Barbara was not the result of that union, cut short by his own murder. But she almost might as well have been. There was much of Veronica in her, and Slade had never known her father, so to him she was like an extension of the woman he'd loved. And it seemd to him that he had known Veronica, and loved her, only days before. The years had passed without his awareness, so it was as if they had never happened. The world had grown older in a flash.

He watched her move through her house like a parent watching a beloved daughter. It was a strange sensation and very unexpected. But not altogether bad.

Barbara studied the big man who sat in her living room. It was hard to believe he was dead, nothing more, really, than a memory made flesh. He had weight, he made noise, he had odor. She was sure that if she tasted him he would taste of the salt and musk of any living man.

She had never been a believer in the supernatural. Ghosts, vampires, werewolves—these were figments, characters from movies that she had no interest in seeing. She never read scary books or watched horror films. The real world was scary enough. She read self-help books and biographies of significant people, and when she went out to a movie it was usually historical or a tearjerker romance, or both.

So she didn't understand how she was supposed

to react to Mike Slade's impossible presence in her life. She thought she should be frightened, but she wasn't. He was not an intimidating person. She could see how he was capable of being so if he chose, but he was always gentle and solicitous with her. He didn't scare her. If he'd been alive, he wouldn't have scared her, and the fact that he was not didn't change that. If anything, it was more like just another fact about him. Brown hair. Blue eyes. Broad-shouldered. Dead.

What was more curious, and more interesting, was the fact that he had been important to her mother. She had saved photographs of him even after marrying her father, and she had spoken fondly of him, though he was long dead by the time Barbara was born. That spoke volumes. She thought her mother must have loved him. She could see, in her mind's eye, her mother tucking herself underneath one of those powerful arms, feeling snug and secure against her hard life. Barbara wondered if her mother might still be alive if this man had not died. Would he ever have allowed the cancer to take her? Or would he have girded his loins and marched into battle against even that?

Of course, Barbara would not have been here to see it. She had loved her father and was glad that he and her mother had fallen in love and had a daughter. But there was something about Mike Slade, some vague sense that maybe her father had been a shadow of him, a somewhat lesser version of the same man, and that was why her mother had fallen for him. He and Slade looked somewhat similar— tall and dark and strong. Barbara remembered her father as a powerfully built man who spoke with gruff candor and loved to laugh. The same seemed to be true of Slade. The creases around his mouth and eyes could have been laugh lines; they deepened when his face broke into one of the few smiles she'd seen.

Now he just looked weary.

"Something happen tonight?" she asked him.

He blinked a couple of times and looked at her. "I got shot at," he said. "I shouldn't tell you—you'll probably turn me in to your pals on the force."

"If I was going to do that, don't you think I would already have done it?" She sounded hurt by the suggestion.

"Probably. Can I trust you, Barbara?"

"Looks that way," she agreed. "I couldn't say why. But there it is."

He nodded. "I went after Wechsler."

"You did what?"

"I couldn't get to see him in his office. So I figured out where he lived, and I went there tonight. But he was ready for me. There were cops everywhere. They spotted me . . . well, someone did." Slade didn't want to tell Barbara that he was certain his attacker was a demon. Bad enough to make her deal with his own presence here. He went on. "He didn't look like a cop, really, but some guy, way out behind Wechsler's house. He came at me, and I shot at him. Then the other ones, the real cops, heard the gunfire and they came after me with their lights and their guns. I had to scram outta there quick."

"So he knows you're after him now."

"Seems to."

"Do you think he knows why?"

"You mean, does he know it's me? I don't know. I can't figure how he would. He knows it's someone, though."

"What are you going to do?" she asked him.

He rubbed his temples with his thumbs as though he had a headache. *Do the dead hurt?* she wondered.

"I don't know yet," Slade said. "That's why I'm here. I need a place to think for a while, try to come up with a plan of what to do next instead of just barging in and tripping over my big feet like I usually do."

"Do you need to get some rest?" she asked, stifling a yawn. "Because I don't mind telling you, I sure do."

"I don't know. I feel kind of tired. Don't know if I can sleep. And if I do, can I be sure I'll wake up again."

"Are you willing to chance it?"

He thought about that for a moment. "On one condition."

"What's that?"

"If I don't wake up—if you come out here and I'm a moldy old corpse, or if I'm just gone—you'll go after Wechsler."

"I'm not going to assassinate him."

"I don't mean that way. Your way. Legal and aboveboard. You know what he did. Just make sure you can prove it, and bring him down."

"I promise I'll try." She surprised herself by saying it. But she knew it was true.

"Then I'll take a little snooze. Is it okay if I use this couch?" He took his jacket off and folded it up like a pillow.

"Sure, go ahead. I'll be in my room if you need anything."

She yawned again and headed into her bedroom, closing the door softly behind her. Part of her thought she was crazy, going to bed with a virtual stranger in the other room, never mind that he claimed to be the walking dead. But she felt safe with him out there, as if he were some kind of a guardian angel who would watch over her.

And anyway, there was that sleeping pill. Staying awake was really out of the question. She slipped under her covers and closed her eyes.

She felt sleep's fingers tugging at her almost instantly. Her mind was drifting in and out of consciousness, and she was willing it to let go. But something nagged at her, something she had wanted to tell Slade . . .

She fell asleep.

Almost instantly she was dreaming. In her dream there was a castle with tall spires and a moat filled with snapping crocodiles, and the castle was guarded by hundreds of knights wearing fancy armor, carrying big shields and long lances.

And facing the castle, alone, a man with a short, broken-bladed sword and a shield made of wood.

But this man, she could see at a glance, had courage and wisdom and compassion. He would face the creatures of the moat and he would battle the soldiers with their superior weapons and great numbers, and he would get inside the castle and usurp the throne from the wicked king within.

At least, in her dream she believed that.

Then the scene shifted, and instead of a castle on a vast lawn, there were stacks of brown boxes, wrapped in twine and covered with dust and cobwebs.

Seeing those, her eyes snapped open. She was instantly alert.

And terrified. If she went into the other room and he was not there, then what?

Heart hammering, she opened the door. The soft

groan of a sleeping man met her ears. She relaxed a little and went into the living room. Slade was there, on the couch, chest rising and falling as he breathed. He looked every inch a living man.

She touched his shoulder. He started.

"Huh?" he asked suddenly.

"Sorry," she said. "You were sleeping so soundly, I hated to wake you."

He smiled. "But I'm still here."

"So it seems," she said. "Listen, I forgot to tell you something."

"What?"

"I was out so hard, I wasn't even sure if it was a dream or real," she said. "Before you came, there was a phone call. A young lady. She wanted to know about Mom. If Mom had any of your files in storage."

"What did you tell her?" he asked. He sat upright.

"I told her there was nothing that I knew about. Then I hung up on her. It was the middle of the night, and I had no idea who she was."

"Oh. It might've been good if she had kept the files. Maybe there's something in there, something about Betty's case or Wechsler, that would help prove he's guilty."

"Oh, she kept them," Barbara told him. "I lied."

"She did? Are you sure?"

"I pay the storage bill every month, so those files had better be there," Barbara said.

"Give me the address," Slade insisted. "I need to check those out. Right now."

She found it and wrote it on a piece of paper for him. He stuffed it into his jacket pocket and went out the door.

"Good luck," she said after he had gone.

She really meant it.

CHAPTER FOURTEEN

Angel hated being in jail.

He was pretty sure there was no one who actually liked it. Certainly none of the people in the holding cell with him. They were, for the most part, large and dirty and possibly crazed. The place stank. Some of the prisoners complained of being cold or hungry. Angel was neither, but he figured if food ever was served, the menu wouldn't include anything that would interest him.

His shoulder still hurt, but it was getting better. He had convinced the arresting officer that it was only a scrape from diving to the ground. It was already healing when the man looked at it, so the officer was willing to believe the story.

Angel was left in holding for several hours. He had asked, when they booked him, for someone to contact Kate Lockley. He was told they would. And then he waited.

And he waited.

And then he waited some more.

One of his fellow inmates decided he wanted the bench Angel was sitting on. He came over, bent down, put his toothless face in front of Angel's, and growled like an animal.

"Move over," he said, almost under his breath.

"No, thanks," Angel replied calmly.

He put an enormous hand on Angel's shoulder, squeezed hard. "I said, shove off."

"No," Angel reminded him. "You said 'Move over.' "

"I meant get lost."

Angel took the man's wrist in his hand and applied pressure. The man's face blanched. His mouth fell open. He tried to move his hand away but couldn't.

Angel released the man before the bones in his wrist were ground to dust.

"Just find another seat," Angel said. "This one's taken."

It wasn't that Angel didn't want to give up the bench. It was just that he didn't want anyone to think he could be *made* to give up the bench. He knew showing weakness in here would be the worst thing he could do. He would become prey to the human predators who surrounded him.

He had been a predator himself, and being on the other side of that equation held no appeal at all.

But after the big man moved away from him, cradling the arm that Angel had quietly almost broken, the others in the holding cell left him alone. Which was just the way he wanted it. He had no interest in making friends with these men.

After three hours that seemed more like three years, a guard came to the cage door and called him. He was allowed to step through and was taken out to a releasing desk where he had to sign some forms. He was told that there would be no charges against him, and he was free to go. His belongings were returned to him in a box. He opened it, took out his carefully folded black leather duster, and put it on. Beneath the coat was a sealed envelope containing the things that had been in his pockets. He ripped it open, tossed the envelope in the trash, and replaced his things, then stepped out into the darkness.

"I told you to be careful," Kate Lockley said. She stood next to her car, in front of the police station, wearing a long camel's-hair coat. Her blond hair fairly glowed in the light that fell from a nearby streetlamp. She smiled, showing even white teeth. "Have fun in there?"

"I'll never look at zoos the same way again," Angel told her.

"I'm sure you won't." She looked at him as he came down the steps toward her. He couldn't quite read what was in her eyes.

"Well?" she asked.

"What?"

"Aren't you going to say it? Tell me I was right?"

"Oh, about being careful? I was careful. Just not careful enough. But thanks for springing me."

"Who says I sprang you?"

"Who else?"

She flashed a quick smile at him. "Okay, I did. Don't ask me why. Part of me—a big part—wanted to see you spend some time in there. Your disregard for the law has been staggeringly flagrant at times."

"Why didn't you leave me there, then?" he asked.

"I'm not sure," she said. She inclined her head toward her car. "Can I give you a ride? I had your car taken back to your place."

"Thanks again."

She unlocked the doors and slid in behind the wheel. Angel went around to the passenger side and climbed in next to her.

"I gave some thought to what you were doing in there," Kate said as she put the car in gear and drew away from the curb. "Whoever this guy is, he's definitely got it bad for Mr. Wechsler. I'd be interested to know if there's a reason for it—and what the connection with the detective's body is."

"Me too," Angel agreed. "There's definitely a connection. I just can't quite see it yet."

"Keep looking," Kate told him. Her tone was almost that of a superior instructing a subordinate.

She shot him a sidelong glance. "Just . . . be careful this time. Carefuller."

Angel chuckled. "Got it."

Kate fell silent, concentrating on her driving and, Angel assumed, turning the case this way and that in her head, like a jeweler inspecting a diamond from every angle before offering an appraisal.

There were plenty of angles to consider. One of the most disturbing, which Angel had tried to avoid looking at, was that the man who shot him had called him a demon. Why? Angel didn't like to think of himself in those terms, but he knew there were those who lumped all vampires into that category.

But for most people—even if, in the dark and the excitement, they had noticed that his features were something other than strictly human—would have thought "vampire," not "demon." What made Slade different?

The point, though, was that Slade, if that's who it was, had recognized Angel's true nature. If the P.I. had been merely human, he could not have done so.

Which made Slade something other than human too.

That fit in with the facts, such as they were, he knew. A long-dead private investigator suddenly shows up and chases around town, trying to find a city official who was alive when the P.I. was killed.

The chances of it being someone impersonating Slade were reduced greatly by this seemingly impossible act of recognition on Slade's part. A real ghost might have some kind of second sight that would let him recognize Angel's nature.

"Wechsler," he said suddenly, the name flitting across his consciousness like a night bird across the moon.

"What about him?" Kate asked.

"In 1961, when Slade was killed, what was Wechsler doing? Has he been in politics that long, or was he in business or what?"

Kate considered for a moment. "I'm not sure."

"There might be some significance to it," Angel suggested. "If Slade is after him, maybe there's a reason. And that reason would have to date back to the sixties."

"Slade's dead."

"That's a given," Angel assented. "But there's this guy who seems to be Slade. Is he trying to run Wechsler down for something that happened way back then?"

"Not being old enough to know specifically what everyone in Los Angeles was doing at that time, I can only say I have no idea. But it may be worth looking into."

"That's what I was thinking."

"Are you thinking that Wechsler might be less than pristine?"

"I'm sure he's as pure as the driven snow," Angel

said with a smile. "But this is Los Angeles, right? City officials have a reputation to live up to. And it hasn't always been a clean one."

"That's putting it mildly," Kate snorted. "If you're going to start digging around in municipal politics, Angel, wear hip boots. You'll need them. And another thing."

"Yeah?"

"Remember what I said about being careful? Be more than that. This city is well known for the reformers it's chewed up and spat out."

She pulled the car over to the curb in front of his building. His Plymouth Belvedere GTX was parked there. "Keys are supposed to be in your office," she said.

He thanked her for the ride and went up the stairs and inside. The place was silent. He had known that Doyle would not be here, since the Irish half-demon was spending the night at the cemetery keeping an eye on Betty McCoy. But he did expect Cordelia. She was doing research on Mike Slade, and usually when she worked into the night, she crashed on the couch or sometimes in Angel's bed, in which case he took the couch.

Tonight she was nowhere to be seen.

That worried him.

What if Slade had not simply recognized him for what he was? What if he knew who Angel was and had come here to finish the job he'd started in the hills behind Wechsler's house? He could have Cordy somewhere.

The office showed no sign of a struggle. The door had been locked when he came in. The keys to the GTX were on Cordy's desk, as Kate had indicated they would be. Everything seemed to be in its place. If Slade had come here, he'd been gentlemanly about it and Cordy had gone along willingly.

Of course, the barrel of a gun could make people more willing than they might otherwise be.

The computer on Cordelia's desk was still on, its screen showing only the colorful wallpaper she had downloaded from someplace. Next to the keyboard was a notepad. A sheet had been torn off it and left lying on the desk, upside down. Angel turned it over. Two names were written on it in Cordy's hand: Barbara Morris and Vic Morris. Neither meant anything to Angel.

Then he saw that there had been another sheet on top of the notepad. He matched the edge of the sheet with the Morris names on it to the slight bit of edge left over when she had torn it off. She had written these names first, then ripped that sheet off and written something on a second sheet. This second sheet, she had pulled off and taken with her.

Angel tried one of the oldest tricks in the book. *This never really works,* he told himself. He picked up her pencil and, using the edge, rubbed gently across the face of the next sheet down.

A name and address appeared.

Well, maybe sometimes, he thought.

Valley U-STOR showed up on the paper, in Cordy's handwriting. Beneath it was an address off Ventura Boulevard in Sherman Oaks.

She had written this down in an excited hurry, pressing hard enough on the paper that it indented the sheet below it. Then she had taken it with her. There was some slight chance that she had simply gone home to her own apartment to get some sleep. He could call, just to check.

But it didn't seem likely.

Why would she take the address of a storage facility home with her?

She wouldn't, he knew. Which meant she had considered this important enough to go out, by herself, in the middle of the night, to check it out.

Which meant it would still be a while before Angel turned in. He scraped the GTX's keys off the desk and into his hand.

CHAPTER FIFTEEN

Harold Wechsler waited in his three-car garage while Barry Fetzer brought the Town Car around. Cars had been coming and going all night, so chances were the police would pay no special attention to this one on the way out. Every car was checked on the way in, but this one would be beneath anyone's notice—the police knew Barry by now, and there would be no one else inside it.

On the way out, though, Wechsler would be in the back seat, hunkered down beneath a blanket.

This night, of all nights, he could ill afford to be trapped in his own house. But this night was the one the lunatic Slade had chosen to attack him in his own home. Which had, in turn, drawn the attention of what seemed like every cop in the city. So on the night that he most needed freedom of movement, he was virtually a prisoner.

In spite of a criminal career spanning decades, Wechsler had never spent a day in jail. He had a knack for not getting caught. And as soon as he'd been able, he'd translated his wealth and power into legitimate businesses. He hadn't been like so many other felons, refusing to pay taxes, trying to bribe law officers and judges. For him, crime had been simply a means to an end, a way to amass wealth quickly. The wonderful part of it was that once he had amassed a small fortune he was able, through perfectly legal means, to turn it into a large fortune. The wealth-building process had always favored those who had wealth to begin with.

The confinement inside his sprawling modern house was wearing on him. But more significantly, this was a very special night, and it was disappearing rapidly.

He couldn't wait any longer.

Fortunately, the garage light flicked on and the door began to rise. Barry was finally pulling the big car in. Wechsler stepped back behind a stack of boxes, so that any random cops peering in would have a harder time seeing him.

Barry pulled the Lincoln in and immediately hit the opener button again. The big door closed. Harold Wechsler opened the rear passenger door and climbed in. Barry swiveled his head around and smiled at his employer.

"Blanket's there, Hal," he said.

"I see it."

"Big night."

"The biggest. Any problems coming in?"

"None at all. One of the cops kind of gave me a funny look, since I only left a little while ago in a different car. But he just waved me through."

"Good. Drive."

Wechsler tucked himself into the footwell—good thing the Lincoln had plenty of room—and pulled the dark blanket over him. The rear windows were tinted, so someone would have to look really hard to know that there was anything or anyone back there.

He felt the car back smoothly out of the garage and turn around in the wide drive. Barry cruised slowly past the police officers ringing the house, and then opened it up once they were out on Leona. The left onto Benedict was a bit of a lurch, but by that point he knew they were beyond any prying eyes. He threw the blanket off and sat up on the backseat.

"Any news from Laine or Reyes? Have they located Slade?"

"No, not yet. They're out there looking. It's a big city."

"It's a big city, but he's a dead P.I. How hard could he be to find?"

"They're looking, Hal."

"They'd better find him before he finds me again."

"No one's going to find you, Hal. You're free and clear."

"Let's hope so."

"We've worked for this for too long. You have."

"You don't need to tell me how long it's been," Wechsler said. He settled back into the comfortable leather and closed his eyes.

And remembered the book.

Los Angeles in 1956, when he had followed the sun here from Kansas City, had been a very different place. The sun seemed to shine every day from a clear blue sky. Waves crashed into the shore, and a few young people had picked up a craze that had started across the sea, on the island of Hawaii, and begun surfing. Others cruised up and down Hollywood and Sunset in their cars. All the boys had short hair and letter jackets, all the girls were blond, fit, and lovely.

Hal Wechsler hated them all.

He was dark and short and scrawny. Surfing seemed an impossible task, requiring balance, coordination, and strength. Unable to afford a car, he'd stolen a bike from a younger kid in the neighborhood, even though he thought he looked stupid and juvenile riding it. Girls didn't look twice at him. He bought a leather jacket, greased his hair back, and tried to hang out with the hoods, but even they rebuffed him, saying he wasn't strong enough, couldn't fight well enough.

He wasn't even accepted by the other demons he met.

Back home, his family had always tried to pass for human. They went out in the daytime, wearing their human faces like badges of honor. They had turned their backs on their own kind. They walked and talked like humans as if it were somehow more noble than embracing their true nature.

And even though Hal didn't agree with that— even though he longed to unleash his inner demon and wreak havoc in the human world—the few other demons he came into contact with wouldn't believe that. He wasn't used to strutting his demon stuff. He had moved on the fringes of Kansas City's criminal community, but always in his human guise.

Arriving on a train from the Midwest, he found a small cottage on a graveled courtyard off Alvarado. To pay the rent, he stole from stores, lifted purses at bus stops, shook down kids for their lunch money.

He was alone in the city of sunshine and second chances. The city where people came to remake themselves in their own desired image.

He determined to remake himself. And when he was done, people would pay attention. People would have to take notice.

He started haunting the used-book stores along Hollywood Boulevard, escaping into fantasies of other worlds and other times. He read Heinlein, Asimov, Bradbury. After a while, the shiny science fantasies soured for him, and he turned to other books, darker, grittier ones: fantasies by Robert E. Howard and Clark Ashton Smith, horror stories by H. P. Lovecraft and Arthur Machen and August Derleth. These stories featured strange magic and sinister elder gods that young Hal Wechsler found tremendously compelling. These stories rang true for him, where the others never did.

So he sought out, and discovered, other stores . . . stores where the books about magic and dark sorcery weren't classified as fiction. He stole when he had to, borrowed when he could, bought when absolutely necessary.

And none of it ever panned out. None of it worked for him. He absorbed Crowley, Bacon, Agrippa, Eliphas Levi. Nothing.

He couldn't understand it.

He knew these people weren't frauds or charlatans. They were magicians. Powerful ones. What they accomplished was far and away beyond what normal straight society could accept.

But nothing worked for Wechsler.

Until he found the book.

It was called *The Path to Power*. It had been written by Jules Lefler, a French Canadian who had taken in the precepts of the magicians who had come before him and there, on the frozen Canadian wasteland, had learned new things that no one else had discovered.

These things worked for Lefler.

And after Wechsler read the book several times and put its principles to the test, they worked for him as well.

He took the book home and spent four days reading it from cover to cover. He would put it down, go into his kitchen to find something to eat, and then would return to it again. He couldn't stop thinking about it—the promise it seemed to offer.

The dark forces he would be unleashing, if it lived up to its promise.

After four days of little sleep and less food, he tried a simple test. In the living room of his small rented cottage he followed the directions for one of the spells. He mixed a few ingredients in a copper bowl, stationed lit candles at intervals around the room, and spoke the required words.

Smoke billowed from the bowl, taking on the form of a beautiful woman. Her eyes were wide and luminous, with galaxies inside them. She told him a secret.

It worked.

He set out to try everything in the book. And in so doing, he became aware of worlds within worlds that he had heard whispered of but never dared to hope were true.

Suddenly he had a new set of acquaintances. He moved in different circles. The city's magic-users opened their doors to him. And as he gathered power about him, other doors opened—doors to the criminal community.

And the outcast, the friendless young man who haunted the bookstores on his stolen bicycle, began to develop a single overriding ambition . . .

Harold Wechsler, sitting in the comfortable seat in back of the Lincoln, began to snore.

"You must be Doug," Cordelia said.

He sat in the office of Valley U-STOR with his feet up on the desk and a truck magazine opened in front of his face. His arms were powerful, his chest deep, his shoulders broad. *Football or wrestling,* Cordelia thought. *Maybe both.* For a moment her inner cheerleader was drawn to the fore. *This guy could be a champion of some kind,* she thought. *And he's wasting his time here. And now I have to twist him around my little finger.*

Such a shame.

At the sound of Cordelia's voice, Doug let out a gasp, swept his feet off the desk, and slammed the magazine down. Then he looked at Cordelia.

Her yellow V-neck top and black DKNY drawstring pants worked their magic. The young man looked, and then looked again, his mouth partly open. Cordelia guessed that women didn't usually drop by in the middle of the night, especially women who looked as good as she knew she did. *Imagine what would have happened if I'd changed before I came over,* she thought.

She graced him with her widest smile. He returned it. His features were broad and friendly. Long brown hair hung over his eyes, and he had developed a habit of shaking his head to clear them frequently. He did this a couple of times while he stared at Cordelia.

Finally he remembered his voice. "Yeah, I'm D-Doug," he managed.

"I'm Cordelia. We talked on the phone."

"Th-that's right," he stammered.

"I did mention I might be dropping by, didn't I?" she asked innocently, knowing full well she had said no such thing.

"Uh, maybe. You might have."

"It's okay, isn't it?" she asked.

"Sure," he said.

"We were talking about my mom's stuff. Veronica Chatsworth. Remember?"

He looked confused for a moment, and then blinked. "Oh, she's your mom?"

"She was." Cordelia allowed her lower lip to tremble just a touch. "She's passed on. Aunt Barbara pays the storage bills now."

"Barbara," the young man repeated.

"Barbara Morris."

"That's right," Doug said, as it dawned on him. "I remember."

"I knew you would," Cordelia said. She walked closer to the desk, perched on a corner of it. "But there's a tiny little problem."

He straightened up, as if the ability to solve her problem would require a very strong and manly individual with military posture. "What is it?" he asked.

Cordelia made her voice small and helpless-sounding, annoying even herself. She was amazed that boys fell for this stuff. "Aunt Barbara can't seem to find her key. She's kind of, you know, blond. We've turned her house upside down, but that key doesn't seem to be anywhere."

"That's no problem," Doug said. "All she needs to do is bring in a picture I.D. We'll get a locksmith to break into her space for her, and then she can put a new lock on."

"That's great," Cordelia said enthusiastically. "Except, oh, there's still one more problem."

"What else?"

"Well, she's in New York. For a month. And she needs something that's in storage. I'm supposed to ship it to her first thing in the morning. That's why I was looking for her key."

"Only the person whose name is on the account is supposed to be able to go in," Doug said officiously.

"I know, Doug, I really do. And if this wasn't the most dire emergency I wouldn't even ask. I'd hate to do anything that might get you into trouble with your boss or anything. Like I said on the phone, I know this is kind of a management decision to make."

"But if you don't have the key, there's really not much I can do. I can call a locksmith, but he's going to charge you an arm and a leg, this time of night."

"I really don't have time to wait for one anyway," Cordelia pouted. "Isn't there some other way?"

"Well, we could cut off the padlock. We have bolt cutters. But you'd have to have another lock to replace it with."

"You must have some spare locks around here," she said.

He tugged open a drawer. "Yeah, there are a couple in here." He came out with a big brass padlock, a key sticking out from its bottom.

"You're a lifesaver," Cordelia said.

"Do you know the space number?" Doug asked her.

"No, Barbara didn't tell me that, and you didn't mention it when I called earlier. You can look that up, right?"

"Sure, no prob," he said. He turned to the computer on his desk, tapped some keys. "Fourteen-twelve," he said after a moment.

"Lead the way," Cordelia suggested.

Doug rose from the desk, crossed to a flat-gray metal locker, and opened it. From inside he took a big bolt cutter, red-handled and heavy-duty. "We'll need this," he announced.

"It's okay for you to be away from the desk for a few minutes, isn't it?" Cordelia asked, voice dripping with concern. "I'd hate to get you in trouble."

"I can't stay away for very long, but a few minutes is fine," he said. "No one comes around at night anyway." He glanced at her. "Well, hardly anyone."

"Guess this is my lucky night," Cordelia said, thinking, *your lucky night, I mean.*

"Yeah," Doug agreed. He led the way out of the office. The storage units were in tall, blank-faced buildings, with alleys running between them just barely wide enough for two cars to pass. Bare lightbulbs mounted high on the walls illuminated the whole facility.

Doug took her two buildings away from the office, to building fourteen. Space twelve was midway down the block. A rolling corrugated-steel door, wide enough for a car, closed it off from the world.

Doug looked at the lock.

"Combination," he said. "Not even a key lock."

"No wonder she didn't know where the key was," Cordelia said with a giggle. "Like I said, blond."

"You think she'd remember the combination if you called her?"

"I can't call her. It's, what, three hours ahead there already? She'd freak out if she knew this thing wasn't already on its way to her."

"Okay," Doug said. "Just checking."

He clamped the big jaws of the bolt cutter around the U-shaped shackle of the padlock. He shook the hair away from his eyes, caught her gaze, and smiled. He flexed his strong arms a little more than was absolutely necessary to work the cutter, and she allowed herself to admire his build as he did so.

The lock broke with a snap.

"There you go," he said. "You're in."

"Thank you so much, Doug," she said, touching his shoulder. "I don't know what I would have done if it hadn't been for you."

"No problem," he said. He handed her the new padlock. "Put this on the door when you're finished in there."

"Right," Cordelia said. "That's what I'll do. I'll put that on." She was suddenly nervous. She had figured out how to get this far, and it had all worked according to plan.

What she hadn't anticipated was what might be inside.

A dead body? A severed head? Boxes of musty old papers that would make her sneeze? Bugs?

"I'd better get back to the office," Doug told her.

"Okay," she said, letting her fingers trail down his arm. "I'll come back by before I leave."

"That'd be great."

She let him walk away. When he was out of sight, she slipped the broken lock from the hasp, took a deep breath, and slid up the rolling door.

Doug walked reluctantly back to the office. *That girl is hot,* he thought. He would have loved to stay with her. Maybe give her a hand moving stuff around in the storage locker until she found what she was looking for. Maybe let her hold his arm a little more.

But if the phone rang or if someone showed up to be let in while he wasn't at the desk, he'd hear about it in the morning. Twenty-four hours is twenty-four hours, his boss was used to saying. The Manfred family had owned this place since it was built during the postwar building boom in southern California, and Owenn Manfred, the grandson of the original owner, was a stickler for detail. He had never done anything, Doug figured—or even imagined doing anything—other than running the family storage business.

That didn't exactly encourage imaginative thinking, Doug knew. To Owenn, rules were rules and were made to be obeyed without question. Exceptions didn't exist. But Doug had been making exceptions ever since the girl had walked into his office, and he knew he'd do it again in the same situation.

He didn't plan to be in the storage business forever. He could play sports, and he could trick out pickup trucks. He was going places.

When he reached his desk, he picked up the magazine he'd been reading, opened it up to the article on installing aftermarket winches that he'd been halfway through. He was thinking about putting a winch on his Frontier.

He didn't even see the man standing in the corner.

The man moved swiftly and silently, slipping a black leather blackjack out of his pocket. He drifted up behind the young man, who was so engrossed in his magazine that he didn't even turn until the blackjack whistled through the air toward his ear. When it hit he gave a low groan and slumped forward onto his truck magazine.

Mike Slade checked the young man's pulse at his neck. He'd be fine. He'd have a headache and a nasty bruise when he came to. But he'd be right as rain, and he'd have a story to tell.

Whoever was digging around in Mike Slade's past wouldn't be so lucky.

CHAPTER SIXTEEN

It shouldn't come as a surprise, Cordelia reflected, *that a bunch of stuff put into storage back in the Dark Ages should be dusty, spiderwebbed, and smell like the inside of the locker that belonged to the girl that no one would talk to because her mother made her wear those thick-soled shoes and funny sweaters and she never showered with the rest of the class.*

As soon as Cordelia was inside, she couldn't wait to get out.

But there was a problem with that. She had driven down here in the middle of the night, sweet-talked Doug, which, to tell the truth, hadn't been all that difficult to do, and gotten access to the storage unit because she wanted to see if there was anything in Mike Slade's personal effects that could be construed as a clue.

This Nancy Drew stuff would be kind of fun, she thought, *if only it involved investigating places that smelled more pleasant. And the hours could be better.*

Since she didn't want to spend all of whatever was left of the night in this place, she went right to work.

The unit was two stories tall, with an unfinished wooden staircase leading up to a loft-like second floor. Downstairs, draped with sheets and cobwebs, was all the furniture that must have come from Slade's office and home. There were a couple of old brown wooden desks, some lamps, a twin bed standing on end, its mattress lashed to it with yellowed, frayed rope. Filing cabinets, also wooden, stood against the back wall. In one corner, arranged almost as they must have been in Slade's living room, were a sofa, two chairs, and a kidney-shaped coffee table, all underneath moth-eaten white sheets. No one had sat on those chairs for decades, Cordelia was sure. The storage fee was paid regularly, by "Aunt Barbara," but no one came here.

She climbed the first few steps and looked up toward the loft. It seemed to be all boxes up there, stacked on top of one another in unsteady piles. Probably his personal things—clothes, dishes, and so on. When he disappeared, Cordelia guessed, no one had known if he was coming back or not, so someone had boxed everything up and put it here just in case. Had there been a body, this stuff might have all been sold at an estate sale. But with no body, it was all still here, more or less untouched if one didn't count whatever insects were able to make their way in.

She decided to start with the file cabinets. With any luck, Slade would have kept them nicely alphabetical and she could just open the *M* cabinet, pull out the Betty McCoy file, and be on her way.

They were empty.

She tried every drawer.

All the same.

When Veronica Chatsworth, or whoever, had emptied the office, she had been thorough.

Cordelia took a quick look in the desk drawers. Empty.

So everything was in boxes, upstairs. She climbed up. The temperature in the loft area seemed ten degrees warmer than downstairs. Close and stuffy.

The smell was different too, the dry dusty smell of old cardboard. Most of the boxes were about the same size and shape, as if they'd been acquired from a moving company.

Brown corrugated cardboard.

Unlabeled.

Cordelia dug into her purse, came up with her car keys. She didn't have a knife, but the key was sharp enough to cut through the brittle twine around the boxes. She started at one corner, ripped into the top box, folded back the flaps. Socks: white, black, powder blue, brown, an argyle that might actually be trendy again. And underwear. Slade was a boxers man. Not exactly a clue, but she mentally filed the information away just the same. She folded the flaps closed, hoisted that box from the stack, opened the next one. Shirts. *These would bring a fortune at some vintage clothing emporium on Melrose,* she thought.

Not that I'd ever sell a dead man's clothes myself. She moved on.

Next box was more clothes. Many pairs of brown pants, folded neatly.

There was beginning to be a pattern to this. Instead of continuing to work through that stack, she turned to a different one. There was no way to distinguish one from another without opening boxes, so just in case the office stuff was all stored at a different end of the room from the home stuff, she crossed to the farthest stack and broke the twine there. Unfolded the flaps.

A bachelor's pots and pans. Someone had scrubbed them before they were boxed up, but they were still stained, their copper bottoms black with age and crust.

"Ewww," Cordelia said as she closed that box.

It was heavy, but she put it on the floor and opened the next one. It contained some truly hideous dishes, orange and yellow and white. She put that box aside too.

Clothes over there, dishes over here, she thought. *Is there any office stuff up here at all?*

There has to be, she decided. Some of the furniture downstairs was definitely office furniture. It had all been emptied out. So the things that were in it were either up here, or . . .

Or they were someplace else. Veronica's garage?

If they weren't here, they could be anywhere. They'd had almost forty years to be spread around the globe. Or destroyed.

She picked another stack, still at random. She broke into the box. On top was a smaller box, like a shirt box, full of pens and pencils. Below that, stiff manila board.

File folders.

She set the pencil box aside.

The file folders were in bundles, secured with more of the old twine that was wrapped around the boxes. She scanned the index tabs. They were written in a clean, feminine hand. Last names, none of which meant anything to her. This bundle seemed to be the *A* through *D* names. These were presumably client files, but this batch didn't help, so she set it down unopened and pulled up the next bundle.

This one only went through the letter *I*. And that finished off the box. She tossed the empty carton to the side and tore into the next one.

Bingo.

The second bundle down in this box contained the *M* names. She yanked the twine off.

"McCoy, Betty," was written on the fourth folder from the bottom.

Cordelia opened the file.

There was nothing in it.

"Just put it down, sister," a male voice demanded.

She looked up. He stood there, at the top of the stairs. His suit was old and mussed, his shirt stained, his tie loosened at the neck. He wore a soft fedora and had the look of a man who was rarely seen without his hat. He looked to be just over six feet tall, with a strong jaw, a powerful neck, and wide shoulders. His mouth was set in a thin, grim line, and there were wrinkles around the heavy-lidded pale blue eyes, which seemed to bore into her.

In his hand was a big dark gun.

She put the empty folder down. "Sure. I mean, there's nothing there anyway. It's empty, so why not? Right? Umm, Mr. Slade, I presume?" She tried a wide smile.

He didn't return it.

"What are you doing here, doll baby?" he asked.

"Looking for . . . well, you should get this, right? Being a detective and all? I was looking for clues."

He snorted something that she took to be a laugh. "Clues? To what?"

Cordelia had faced vampires and demons and monsters, with the Scoobs back in Sunnydale, with Angel and Doyle, and on her own. But this guy, staring at her, was something different. He looked human. He sounded human. She had reason to believe that he was something other than human, some kind of ghost or zombie. But then again, he could well be human and crazy, just someone impersonating a long-dead private detective.

Either way, holding that gun, he was terrifying to her.

"Well, to you, I guess. If you are in fact Mike Slade. We've been trying to find you."

"You found me," he said. His words were short, clipped. "Now what?"

"Umm, well, you got me there. I wasn't really thinking that far ahead, if you want to know the truth. That's me all over, poor impulse control. No looking before I leap, and all that."

"And the talking too much? Is that one of your problems too?"

"Aggravated by nerves," she said, nodding her head. "When I'm scared, I have a tendency to, well, babble, I guess you'd call it. Yes, babble is definitely the right word. Like a brook, I babble."

"I get the picture," Slade snapped. "You can knock it off now."

"Knocking. Right away. See me knocking it off?"

He waggled the gun at her, as if to remind her that he still held it. She closed her mouth, and pulled an invisible zipper across her lips in the international "I'm shutting up now" sign.

"So you're trying to find me? And you won't say why, eh? Why's that? Are you in cahoots with Wechsler?"

Cordelia shrugged, tried to look inquisitive.

"What?" Slade asked, anger tinging his voice.

She pointed to her mouth.

"You can talk," he snarled. "Just stick to the point."

"Oh," Cordelia said. "Okay. Fine, then. Umm, I have no idea who Wechsler is."

"Are you being straight with me?"

"Absolutely. I mean, it's possible that Angel mentioned the name. It does sound kind of familiar, now that you mention it. But I couldn't begin to say why. It sounds like one of those names that sound like a lot of other names, you know. Like, Dexter. Or Hexler. Or Shecky."

"I like it better when you don't talk," Slade said.

"Well, you did ask. Anyway, my point is that I couldn't possibly be in cahoots with him, because I don't even know who he is. At this point, I don't even remember the name. Was it Jeckle or Heckle?"

"Wechsler. Harold Wechsler."

"Nope, don't know him."

"And who's this Angel you mentioned?"

"Oh, him. He's kind of my associate. Or my boss. More of a boss, I guess. You'd like him. He's a private investigator, same as you. If you're really Slade, that is, since you still haven't even told me that."

"I'm Slade."

"Well, we got that cleared up, then. And I'm

Cordelia. Cordelia Chase, of Angel Investigations."
She stuck out her hand to shake. He looked at it,
but he didn't move toward her or put the gun away.
After a moment she lowered her hand to her side,
somewhat sheepishly.

"So he's a private eye, huh?" Slade said. "What's
he doing nosing around my business? Who's he
snooping for?"

"As I'm sure you know, we have to keep the
names of our clients strictly confidential, and—"

"As I'm sure *you* know, this is a gun and it fires
bullets. It fires them especially if I'm monkeyed
with or my questions aren't answered."

"Now, see, if Angel would be that forceful, I'm
sure he'd get better results. Especially when it's
time to collect on the bills. I don't imagine you have
deadbeat clients, do you, Mr. Slade?"

"Not for very long," Slade said. "And never more
than once."

"That's what I thought."

"You still haven't answered me, doll baby. Who is
this Angel working for?"

"This is really hard to explain if you don't know
all the background," Cordelia said. She felt that
the words were going to get away from her again.
The gun was making her nervous, and the guy
holding the gun was making her terrified. "But I
guess the short answer is, someone named Betty
McCoy."

He took a quick step toward her, hand raised as if to strike. He didn't, but the glare in his eyes was unmistakably furious. "Be straight with me!"

"I am! All we know about her is her name."

"Betty McCoy's been dead for decades."

"Yeah, and that. We know that part."

"Then how is she his client?"

"Like I said, long story."

"I'm just about out of patience with you, doll baby," he said. He sounded as if his patience was long since gone.

"The name is Cordelia," she reminded him. "And our other associate, Doyle, he gets these visions. From the Powers That Be. He usually gets a name, a face, an address, a situation, something like that. From someone in need. Angel tries to help those people who are in need. But this vision, all it was was a name and address. The name was Betty McCoy, and the address was a cemetery. So we figured out the part about her being dead."

"You must be brilliant detectives."

"Hey, maybe we're not dead, but that doesn't mean sarcasm is called for," Cordelia shot back. "Well, if you don't count Angel, that is."

"Angel's dead?"

"Look, I told you this was a long story. If you don't want me to tell it my way, maybe we should come back to it some other time."

"Never mind," he barked. "What folder is that you were looking at when I came in?"

"Betty McCoy's," Cordelia replied.

"And it's empty?"

"Totally," she said. She gingerly picked it up between two fingers, held it so that it flopped open. "You must have been there long enough to see me find it, so you know I didn't take anything out."

"You're right, you didn't," Slade agreed. "So where do you suppose the documents are? That folder had papers in it the last time I saw it."

"Which was when?"

Slade snapped the fingers of his left hand. "That's it. Wechsler. After he killed me. He must have taken the files."

"So you *are* dead?"

"Of course I am," Slade said, as if explaining something to a child. "What did you think?"

"Well, I assumed, but I didn't know for sure."

"Sounds like you spend a lot of time with dead guys."

"Now that you mention it. Maybe that's part of the problem with my social life."

"If you're really working for Wechsler, sister, your social life is gonna be the least of your concerns."

"You don't listen very well, do you? I don't know Wechsler. There is no one named Wechsler that I know. Not a soul."

"But *you* know Wechsler, don't you, Slade?" another voice asked.

A voice Cordelia recognized.

Angel.

"You tried to kill Wechsler tonight, didn't you, Slade?" Angel went on. "And you shot me."

He had appeared on the railing of the loft, jumping up, in order not to be heard climbing the creaky wooden stairs. Slade whirled, pointed his gun at Angel, who was in full vampire mode.

"I'll do it again, too, demon," Slade said.

"I'm already dead," Angel said. "You're not the only one. Get used to it."

Slade turned the gun away from Angel and pointed it at Cordelia again. "Maybe you are dead," he said. "But she's not."

Cordelia looked down the barrel of the big gun. It was as black as the inside of a grave and seemed as wide and deep.

"Um, Angel? I think maybe he means it."

"I'm sure he does," Angel hissed. He leaped.

Slade fired.

CHAPTER SEVENTEEN

Angel slammed into Cordelia and knocked her sprawling.

She could hear the bullet whistle through the air past her head—past where her head had been, right before Angel broke several of her ribs with his shoulder. She'd have a bruise that would keep her out of crop tops for weeks.

He had landed on top of her, his face—bulging forehead, beady eyes, long sharp teeth—just inches from hers. *Not his best look,* she thought.

"Stay down," he hissed.

The next moment his weight was off her and he was flying through the air toward Slade. The gun went off again, and Cordelia heard wood splinter in the rafters overhead.

She stayed low.

*   *   *

Angel hurled himself at Slade. The guy might be dead—probably was, it seemed—but he had felt solid earlier tonight. So had his bullet, even though it didn't feel as if it was still there.

He figured he owed the man something.

He plowed into Slade, knocking him backward into a stack of boxes. The boxes collapsed, and Slade fell in a heap among them. He squeezed off another shot, which went wild. Then he clawed his way to his feet. Angel let him almost regain his balance before delivering a spinning kick. His foot caught the P.I. in the solar plexus. The man doubled over around the kick, his gun flying away. Angel completed the spin, his other foot lashing out and connecting with Slade's jaw. The P.I. went down again.

But as quickly as he did, he came back up.

Many men—mortal men—would have been completely undone by two of Angel's most powerful kicks. This guy just shook them off and came back for more.

So he is dead. Just as we figured, Angel thought.

Problem being, how did one fight him? Staking him probably wouldn't work.

So Angel decided to keep hitting until he got results.

But the detective was faster than he anticipated.

This time, instead of struggling to his feet, he lunged at Angel from his spot on the crushed boxes. His fists found Angel's midsection. One crushing blow after another landed. Angel caught Slade's shoulders and shoved him back and away, but he'd taken some damage.

Now they were both hurting.

Slade came at him again. His fists flew, one nailing Angel just below the left eye. Angel saw a red flash and felt his skin break.

He punched back, one hand landing on Slade's ear. Slade staggered. Angel pressed the advantage, pummeling Slade mercilessly.

Slade felt solid, but Angel couldn't tell that he was doing any actual harm. Slade didn't seem to be slowed by the assault. He grunted, and he sometimes seemed to have the wind knocked out of him, but never for long. He always came back swinging.

Angel couldn't remember ever having had this hard a fight.

He was giving it everything he had. He tried karate, kung fu, good old-fashioned street fighting—everything he'd learned in more than two hundred years of knocking about the globe.

Slade just shook it off, and kept dishing out his own kind of punishment.

The more blows he landed on Angel, the more Angel began to worry that he might finally have met someone he couldn't outlast. It wasn't a cheerful sensation.

Slade doubled his fists together and brought them arcing toward Angel's chin. Angel blocked, but ineffectively. The detective's doubled fists battered past his hands and slammed into his jaw.

He fell.

"Not going well for your guy, is it?"

Cordelia spun. A woman—slim and fit, with shiny brown hair pulled back into a ponytail—stood looking at her from the top of the stairs. She wore a T-shirt and jeans with a dark blue windbreaker.

"Don't worry about my guy," Cordelia replied. "He can take care of himself."

"Maybe," the woman said. "But from here it doesn't look as if he's doing that great."

"Look, I don't know who you are or what you're doing here, but this is kind of a private thing," Cordelia said. "So maybe you should just take your opinions and go find someone else to share them."

"I have as much right to be here as anyone," the woman said. "Considering I'm the one who pays the bills on this place."

Cordelia looked at her again, eyes wide.

"Oh, my God," she said. "You're Aunt Barbara?"

"What?" the woman asked.

"Never mind," Cordelia quickly said. "You're Barbara Morris?"

"That's right," Barbara said. "How do you know my name. Who are you? And who's that?"

"Do you think you could hold it to one question

at a time?" Cordelia pleaded. "I can only talk so fast. And I'm trying to watch the fight."

"Why? Do you like seeing your boyfriend get his head handed to him?"

"He's not my boyfriend," Cordelia replied.

"I can see why," Barbara said. "Seems to have a good build, but those facial deformities kind of spoil the look."

"For your information," Cordelia snapped, "he's . . . well, never mind what he is. Anyway, why do you care? Are you dating the other guy?"

"Of course not!" Barbara shot back. "He's old enough to be my grandfather."

"Doesn't look it from here."

"That's because—"

"Oh, right. Because he's a corpse."

"You know about that?"

"What do I look, stupid?" Cordelia asked. "That's a rhetorical question, so don't even think about answering it. And also, I remember now . . . Your mother used to work for him, right? Was she sweet on him? I'm thinking they were a thing, you know."

"They might have been, but it was all before I was born," Barbara said. "How do you know all this?"

"I've been doing some digging," Cordelia said. She watched Angel take a couple of swings at Slade. He connected, and Slade grunted but didn't fall down.

"Into me? Or him?" Barbara asked. "And what's up with that guy? He doesn't look entirely human, you ask me. Those teeth . . ."

"Okay, he's a vampire, all right?" Cordelia said. Barbara looked at her, eyes like saucers. "Oh, like you aren't hanging around with a dead guy of your own."

"I guess we do have that in common," Barbara said. "Dead guys."

"Older dead guys, if you want to get specific," Cordelia pointed out.

"But you don't . . ."

Cordelia made a face. "Of course not! Not that he's not hot. But still."

"I know what you mean," Barbara agreed.

Angel lifted a box over his head and slammed it down into Slade. It couldn't have weighed more than thirty pounds, so he doubted it would have much impact. But he was running out of ideas.

Slade took a couple of steps back. Angel feinted with a right, and when Slade brought his hands up to block, Angel drove in with a left jab. Slade lost another step. Angel followed that with a combination, left-left-right, and then two more rights in quick succession. Slade fell back more.

As long as he doesn't figure out what I'm doing, Angel thought, *I should be able to end this.*

He continued to press, continued to drive Slade back step by step, inch by inch. His fists hammered

Slade nonstop. With every blow he was closer to his goal.

And finally he was there.

Slade was inches from the railing that surrounded the loft. The railing was a two-by-two nailed to a series of two-by-four supports. But it didn't look strong, and that was what Angel was counting on.

As weary as he was, he doubled his efforts, fists raining into Slade. The private eye took one more step backward, and he was up against the rail.

Angel leaped straight up, caught hold of a rafter with both hands, and kicked out with his feet.

Slade crashed through the railing and went over the side.

He landed down below with a huge racket.

"I told you he was doing okay," Cordelia said.

"Guess you're right. It sure looked like he was on the losing end before," Barbara said. She didn't seem too concerned, though.

"You're not worried about Slade?"

"Of course not. He's already dead. What can happen to him?"

"Good point." If he'd been a vampire, he could have gotten dusted, but Cordelia wasn't going to point that out, in case it was something that Slade didn't know about. And she wasn't sure if the reverse was true, if there was anything that Angel could do that would finish Slade off once and for all.

"So what's the deal with him, anyway?" Cordelia asked. She felt that maybe she should be trying to help, but she knew Angel could take care of himself, and she would only be in the way. Besides, in case Barbara tried anything, she could . . . well, she'd think of something. "He seems to have anger-management issues."

"I think it has something to do with having been murdered," Barbara said. "I haven't really known him that long. But the murder seems to have had quite an impact on him."

"Makes a certain amount of sense."

"And he's back now, he thinks, because he's supposed to finish the case that he was working on when he was killed."

A light flashed on for Cordelia. "And Betty McCoy was his client?"

"That's right," Barbara said.

"Suddenly things are starting to make sense," Cordelia said. "Angel," she called. "We have to talk."

"In a minute," Angel said. He was looking down the stairs.

And coming up the stairs, with heavy footfalls, was a mussed and dusty Mike Slade.

"No, I think now," Cordelia persisted.

"Cordy—" Angel began.

"We're all on the same side here, Angel. Slade is working for Betty McCoy."

"That's right," Slade said. "What about it?"

"Okay, let's talk," Angel said.

Several minutes later they were sitting downstairs on the sofa and chairs around the freeform plastic coffee table. They had wadded up the sheets that covered the furniture and tossed them into a corner. Mike Slade was talking animatedly, gesticulating as he did. It was the first time he'd had a real audience in—well, it felt like days, but he knew it was really going on forty years.

"I was hired by this dame, Betty McCoy," he was saying. He could see her, in his mind's eye, dabbing at her eyes with a tissue, wrinkling her pert little nose. "Cute young thing. She had short dark hair in kind of a bob, and the longest neck, like Audrey Hepburn's. And she was in a lot of trouble, she said. She was in tears, sitting there in the guest chair in my office."

"What was she there for?" Angel asked.

"She said she'd been robbed," Slade replied. "It turned out to be a lot more complicated than that, but that's what she told me at first. This guy Hal Wechsler had robbed her. I asked how she knew it was him, and that's when she started to cry. I tossed her a handkerchief, gave her a few minutes to pull herself together, and started in again. 'Tell it to me from the beginning, sweetheart,' I told her. 'And don't leave anything out. Nothing you can say will surprise me.'"

"Boy, was I wrong."

"What do you mean?" Cordelia asked him.

"I thought I'd seen it all," Slade explained. "But the story she told shook me to my bones. I'd been living in a dream world. I guess you guys know all about it, but I didn't have a clue.

"Even then, when I told her I wanted to hear the whole story, she only told me parts of it. She told me that she'd met Wechsler at this nightclub she worked at, where she was the cigarette girl."

"The Rialto Lounge," Angel offered.

"That's right," Slade said, surprised. "You are good at this private eye game, aren't you?"

"I do okay," Angel replied.

"She was working at the Rialto, and he used to come in there. He was strictly small time then, she said. But he spent a lot of dough, tipped big. He made her think he was a player in the rackets, on his way up. He had a kind of oily charm, I guess, and she was young and foolish enough to find it intriguing. So they started to go out for drinks or a malted on Saturday afternoons, and before she knew what hit her, he'd moved into her place.

"She was still paying the full rent and buying the groceries, and he was out until all hours working his scams, trying for the big score that would put them both on easy street, he told her. He never gave her details, even when he was gone for days at a time, and she just gave up asking.

"And then he got her hooked on dope."

"Nice boyfriend," Cordelia said.

"Right. Told her she was too tense. He said the dope would relax her, make her feel better about herself. She went along with it, because he sweet-talked her the way he always did. Pretty soon she was using drugs every morning when she woke up, every night before she went to bed, and a couple of times in between."

"What drug was it?" Barbara asked.

"He called it Flux," Slade replied. "That's the only name she ever knew it by. He told her it was something he'd invented himself. She didn't ask questions. The drug made her feel too good to want to question things. Made her feel dreamy, peaceful. At ease. And that was when he robbed her."

"What did he take?" Angel asked. "I can't imagine she had much."

"That was the strange thing, at least at first," Slade said. "She owned a hi-fi, a television, and she had a little cash saved up. He didn't touch those things. But he took some things her grandmother had left her. Some personal items, she said. I asked her what, specifically. She finally told me there was a little basket of things, handed down from her grandmother because her mother had died when she was young. A couple of candles, an incense burner and some incense, a dagger, and a scroll. The scroll, she said, was the most important thing because it was beautiful and because she knew it had been very important to her grandmother, although she didn't know why.

"So I started looking for Wechsler. Digging into his past, trying to find people who knew him. You know how it goes."

Angel nodded.

"But everything I turned up just made the whole case seem stranger and stranger," Slade went on. "People who knew Wechsler just weren't right, somehow.

"And the deeper I dug, the stranger it got. What I found out was that Wechsler wasn't even human—and you gotta understand how hard it was for me to accept this. But a couple of his buddies paid me a visit one day, and when it turned out they had horns and hooves and tails, I started to realize just what I was getting myself into.

"I went back to Betty, and she tried to tell me just to forget about it, to give it up. It was too late for that, I told her. Finally she confessed that she was a demon, so was Wechsler, and so were a lot of their friends. I told her to prove it to me, and she couldn't. She said since she'd been using Flux, she hadn't been able to change out of her human form. Wechsler had been getting a lot of demons hooked on the stuff, it turned out, and once they began using, they were stuck as humans. Their demon nature subsided, and they lived purely as humans.

Which some of them wanted to do anyway, but most wanted to keep their options open.

"And then, it turned out, they died. They used Flux more and more often, and pretty soon it killed them."

Slade swallowed, hard. He had taken Betty into his apartment while she kicked the habit. Veronica had come over to help. They spent a week there while Betty was alternately sick, angry, tearful, and afraid. By the time the week was over, though, it looked as if she was over the worst of it.

It was a hard week, though. At the end of it, Slade wanted nothing in the world more than Wechsler's throat between his hands.

"Betty got clean," he said, "and since I'd found out about the demon stuff, she told me more about her grandmother. Seems the old lady was a powerful magician in addition to being a demon. The stuff in the basket was some of her magical apparatus, and the scroll was a spell of some kind. Very powerful, she said. Betty had never known exactly what the spell was for, but she guessed that Wechsler probably did, since he was so anxious to get his hands on it.

"The more I dug, the more anxious I was to stop Wechsler. He'd been moving Flux throughout the demon community, which was a lot more widespread than any humans knew. It had the same effect on all of them—it squelched their demon side so that they had to pass as human, and then it killed them. Hundreds of demons were addicted, it turned out. They were hooked. The stuff made them feel so good that they didn't care about the downside."

"That's kind of true of most drugs, isn't it?" Cordelia asked. "If people realized what the stuff was really doing to them, they'd never start in the first place."

"I guess that's true," Slade replied. "At first I saw the stuff only from Betty's point of view, but then I met a lot of other demons as I investigated. Flux was poison, as far as I was concerned. And, demons or not, Wechsler was killing people right and left. He had to be stopped. And I was going to stop him."

"So what happened?" Cordelia asked.

Slade took a deep breath. "That's when he killed me."

CHAPTER EIGHTEEN

"Wechsler is the one who murdered you?" Angel asked.

"That's right," Slade said. "He hid in my office with two of his gunsels and they let me have it when I came in. Didn't even have a chance to pull my own piece. *Bang, bang, bang.* Shot me right there. Then they bricked me up inside my own closet, while Wechsler performed some kind of binding spell to keep me there. I guess he wasn't sure how friendly I might have gotten with some of the demons, and he was afraid I might have made arrangements to be reanimated after my death, just in case.

"Truth is, that hadn't even occurred to me; I didn't know it was an option. But when my office was demolished, I guess reanimation happened automatically. I'm only guessing now, but I think I came back to life because I want Wechsler so much.

It isn't just Betty, and it isn't just that he killed me. It's everything he's done. And now people think he's legit, and he's got a big city job. He's got to be stopped."

"You know Betty died," Angel said softly. "In 1964." He didn't want to upset Slade, but figured the man deserved to know.

"I thought so," Slade said. He looked disheartened. "It's been too long. I hope she went peacefully."

"As far as we know," Cordelia replied. She didn't bother to tell Slade that Betty had started using drugs again. Somehow she thought that knowing that would only hurt him. "Although I don't think her spirit is quite at rest yet. I think that's why our friend Doyle had a vision about her. When you were released from the binding spell, it stirred her in some way. Because she knew you had come back to bring her peace."

"That's what I've been trying to do," Slade said. "I've been trying to get Wechsler since I came back." He looked pointedly at Angel. "If you hadn't been at his place tonight, I might have gotten him then."

"There were too many police there," Angel said. "I didn't want them to get hurt. Or you. Or Wechsler. Although knowing what I know now, I'd be a little less concerned about him."

"Just don't get in my way next time he's in my sights," Slade insisted.

"You know, something else makes sense now," Angel said. "Kate Lockley—she's a police detective I know—told me that on the day they found your body, someone who worked in Wechsler's office had been trying to get into the building."

"Probably wanted to do a different kind of binding spell, something to keep me down no matter what."

"That's what I was thinking," Angel agreed.

"If Wechsler knows I'm back, he's probably running scared," Slade suggested.

"So do you think this was his plan all along? To gain legitimacy, a government position, money and power?"

"Sounds like a reasonable goal to me," Cordelia put in.

"I don't know," Slade said. "Seems as if he must have been after more than that. He was addicting and killing hundreds of his own kind. Why would he do that unless there was a big payoff for him at the end of it all? There were easier ways to get money and power, if that was all he wanted."

"So what *was* he after?" Angel wondered.

"I never figured that out. I guess I was getting close, or he wouldn't have killed me."

"Good point," Barbara said, finally speaking up. "That probably means you were too close for comfort."

"That's the way I figure it," Slade said.

"If only we knew what was on Betty's grandmother's scroll," Angel suggested. "Did you ever recover it?"

Slade rose from his chair. "Never found the real thing," he said. He crossed to the empty file cabinets standing against the rear wall. He slid a drawer all the way out, then turned it over. Something was taped to the bottom. He tore off the tape and brought a big piece of paper back to the corner where the others sat.

"Betty made a copy," he went on. "She didn't know what it was all about, but she knew it was precious and beautiful. She wanted to hang the copy on her wall and keep the original someplace safe. I had her give me the copy. This is it."

Angel took the yellowed paper from Slade. "Melechian," Angel announced. "At least, that's what it looks like. Let me see . . ."

"Hey! You there!"

Doyle turned. A flashlight beam blinded him.

He'd been spotted.

"What are you doing here?" the flashlight wielder demanded.

Doyle put his hands up to block the beam. He saw a man coming at him. A guard, in a uniform. He jingled as he ran. Maybe forty pounds overweight, maybe twenty years older than Doyle.

But there was a holster on his belt, and a gun in the holster. And he was reaching for it.

"Hey, listen," Doyle said placatingly. "I was just, you know, payin' my respects to the dear departed."

"Visiting hours are over," the guard snarled.

"Uncle Bob, he never liked daylight much," Doyle offered. "Used to work nights, sleep days. Hated the sun. It just wouldn't seem right, comin' to see him durin' the day. It'd be like wakin' him up for no reason."

"You're trespassing," the guard said. "If you go to prison, you won't have to worry about seeing the sun for a few years. Is that what you want?"

Doyle stepped backward, still holding his hands up, trying not to look like a threat. "No, not at all. Me personally, I love the sun. The beach, you know, convertibles, all that. That's me. I'd be darker than George Hamilton if I had my way. Problem with me is I don't tan, I stroke, you know, that's why I'm a little on the pale side. But otherwise, I'm a real sun worshiper. It's only Uncle John who hated it."

"Thought it was Uncle Bob," the guard said. He drew the revolver at his hip.

"Bob and John both," Doyle backpedaled. "Twins. They worked the graveyard shift at the factory—graveyard, that's a bit ironic, don't you think?"

"What I think, funnyman, is that you ought to be making up your mind pretty fast. You can leave now— I been watching you, and I don't think you've been doing anything, except loitering. Or you can stand there and make wisecracks and I can call in the cops and have you arrested for vandalism, vagrancy, trespassing, and about twenty other things I'll be thinking of while we're waiting for the police."

Doyle didn't have to think for long. Ending up in jail wouldn't help Angel investigate Betty McCoy. He didn't want to leave his post, but it didn't look as if the man with the gun was leaving him the option of sticking around. "You know, of those two choices I think I like the first one better. The one where I leave on my own."

"Thing about me is that I change my mind fast," the guard said. "So if you're not outside that gate, say, by the time I count to twenty or so, I might just change it again."

"I'm going," Doyle assured him. "You don't even see me. I'm gone."

He ran for the main gate, dodging the tombstones as he went. He didn't stop until he was through them. Looking back from the sidewalk, he saw the guard still watching him, and just now holstering his gun.

He'd have to let Angel know he'd been made.

"I'm not fluent in Melechian," Angel was saying. "But I can make out some of this."

"Kind of like me with Spanish," Cordelia said. "I can order a quesadilla, but if it gets more complicated than that, I'm pretty much helpless."

"This is a little more complex than reading a menu," Angel said. "And I think the stakes are a bit higher, if I'm reading this right, anyway."

"What do you think it is?" Slade asked him.

"If I'm right . . . you said this guy is the head of the Department of Water and Power now?"

"That's right," Barbara said. "As of a week or so ago."

"Then this could be trouble," Angel said. "I think we've found out what Wechsler's plan was all along."

"What do you mean?" Slade asked.

"Water," Angel said. "We have to hurry." He started for the door. The others rose and followed him. He led them out the big sliding door and into the narrow alleyway, now clogged with vehicles.

"We'll take my car," Angel announced.

"He likes to be the driver," Cordelia told Barbara and Slade. "It's some kind of guy thing."

They all piled into the Plymouth Belvedere. Slade looked at it admiringly before he slid into the front seat next to Angel. "Plymouth man, eh? Good for you. Finest Detroit can make. There's mine." He pointed at the Fury.

"Classic," Angel said offhandedly, not really looking at it.

"You can say that again," Slade said. "This one's nice, too. Not much chrome, but otherwise it's not bad."

"We need to go where there's a lot of water," Angel said, obviously not paying Slade's auto critique any mind. "Where water comes into the city's system."

"There's a main processing plant, where the water the city brings in is treated before it gets into the system," Barbara said, from the backseat. "It's on the other side of West Covina, in the San Gabriel foothills."

"That's where we're headed, then. It's got to be."

"What about a gat?" Slade asked Angel.

"Sorry?" Angel replied. He made a left onto Ventura, headed for the 134 freeway, which would take them through Glendale and Pasadena, where they'd catch the 210 into West Covina. This time of the night, or morning, there was no traffic and it would be a fast trip.

"A piece. A rod. I pack a Browning .38. Beautiful piece."

"He means a gun," Barbara translated.

"What about it?"

"What do you carry?"

Angel shook his head. "I don't."

"And you call yourself a private dick?"

"Not in those terms, exactly."

"What do you do when you have to plug somebody?"

"I, uh . . . don't do a lot of plugging," Angel said.

Slade shook his head. "I just don't understand how you can get anything done, you don't carry a rod. Can't even pistol-whip a canary who won't sing."

Angel flashed briefly on the collection of weapons he did own—axes, swords, arrows, and of course stakes. Guns just didn't seem to help much against the kind of enemy he usually found himself up against, and in his experience, firearms were more trouble than they were worth.

"I don't often have occasion to pistol-whip anyone," he told Slade. "And guns aren't all they're cracked up to be, anyway. Yours didn't do much damage to me, did it?"

"I was wondering about that," Slade confessed. "But once I found out you were a vampire, then it made sense."

"Tell me this," Angel asked. "When's the last time you reloaded that thing?"

Slade gripped his chin while he thought it over. When he turned back to Angel, he had a searching look in his blue eyes. "I guess I haven't, since I came back to life, I mean."

"That's what I thought," Angel said. "The places you've fired it, people have been hurt if they saw you firing at them. Me included. But no bullets have been found, no shell casings, no physical evidence that any real shooting was done."

Realization dawned on Slade like a light switching on in a dark room. "You're saying it's a phantom gun?"

"Think about it," Angel prompted. "You were dead for thirty-some years. I hate to be blunt, but your flesh must have decomposed, your clothes would have fallen apart. The gun probably would have rusted. Yet when you came back, I assume you were fully dressed. You didn't buy those clothes at a discount store on Hollywood Boulevard. You had money in your pockets, flesh on your bones, and a working gun. The money I can believe, but there's no way the gun would still work. My guess is that the gun is magic, not real, and it only injures people because they believe it will. The mind is a powerful thing, Slade. It can will injuries to a body—even kill a body, maybe, if it's convinced enough. But it can't manufacture little pieces of lead or brass to leave behind."

Slade let out a long, low whistle. "I guess you're right, Angel," he said, a little sadly. "Guess I'm really not here at all, if you look at it that way."

"You're here," Cordelia said. "We're all running around because of you, and I can't tell you how much I'd rather just be sleeping in my own bed tonight than crawling around in your dusty old files."

"Here but not here," Slade agreed. "And for how long?"

Barbara reached out from the backseat and massaged his shoulders. "However long it is, we'll make the best of it," she promised.

Slade put one of his big hands over hers, and squeezed.

Doyle stood outside a bodega, across the street from the cemetery. An occasional car drifted past, but otherwise the street was deserted and quiet. There was a pay phone attached to the bodega's brick wall. Doyle fished a couple of coins from his pocket and shoved them down the slot. He dialed Angel's number, hoping he had his cell phone turned on.

"Yeah," Angel answered on the second ring.

"Angel," Doyle said. He sounded winded. "Hey, man, I've been kicked outta the cemetery."

"Kicked out?" Angel repeated.

"Yeah, I'm callin' from a pay phone. Security guard spotted me hangin' around and gave me the boot."

"Can you see Betty's grave from outside?"

"Not really," Doyle replied. "It's down in a little dip. You pretty much have to be right there to see it."

"Then you have to get back in," Angel said. "I'm not certain yet what's going on, but it's going down tonight, I'm pretty sure."

"That's good, 'cause I don't know if I can take another night of this," Doyle said. "There's demons buried in this place, Angel. Families I've known. Tell you the truth, I wasn't exactly heartbroken to be thrown out of there."

"Get back inside," Angel repeated. "There are only a couple of hours till the sun comes up."

"Got it, Angel," Doyle agreed. "I'm on my way."

He hung up the phone.

For all he knew, the guard was still watching him. Doyle would have been watching if the situation were reversed.

So he had to come up with a way to ditch the guard and get back inside—through the fence or over it—without being spotted. Then he'd have to get close to Betty's grave, find a hiding place, and stay put until the sun came up.

He glanced at his watch. Still a little more than two hours away. What a long night.

And it was not over yet.

He went around the corner from the bodega, away from the cemetery. Once he was out of sight of it, he broke into a jog, around the next corner and down two blocks. Then he came back down toward Sunset. At that corner he stopped, pressed himself flat against the building, and watched the cemetery.

He couldn't see any movement from here.

The guard was in there somewhere. Doyle had thought that he stayed in the little security office near the front gate all night, but apparently that was not really the case. Chances were he was back in there now, but there was no guarantee.

And Doyle had to get across the four lanes of Sunset to get back inside. Traffic wasn't a problem, but the boulevard was a wide open area where he would have no cover. If the guard was still watching the street, he'd spot Doyle.

That was a guarantee.

There was no way around it. Doyle came around the corner quickly, and walked down a quarter of a block so he was at the darkest spot between two streetlights.

Not dark, but darker.

He stepped off the curb, ducked down as low as he could—as if that would help—and dashed across the street. On the other side, he ran up the sidewalk and flattened himself against the cemetery fence.

No flashlight beam struck him in the face. No one fired a gun at him or came at him with a nightstick. He turned and looked back at Sunset. A big old Lincoln Continental, painted a sickly shade of pea green, cruised past with five or six kids inside it, but there was no other motion on the street.

Back to the graveyard. All was still quiet inside, as far as he could tell. Quiet as the grave, he told himself, only half joking. He knew, better than most, that graves weren't always as quiet as the saying implied.

He couldn't risk going back to the main gate. The guardhouse was too close by, and the guard would certainly be keeping an eye on the gate. The fence was made up of tall rods, an inch or more in diameter, spaced about six inches apart, with crosspieces at the top and bottom. At the tops of the rods were spear-point appendages. The rods were too close together for Doyle to slip between them.

That meant he had to go over the fence. He took another quick look at the street. There was no one to see him. He put his right foot up on the lower crosspiece, grabbed two of the rods in his fists, and hoisted himself up. He had to push off the rods with his feet to make upward progress, but the gate wasn't really too hard to climb. At the top, he pulled himself up, got a foot on the top crosspiece, and swung himself over.

Then he dropped down onto the grass, landing in a crouch with a soft thump. He froze, half expecting to hear the guard's voice, or even a hail of bullets. When neither came, he rose.

Back inside the cemetery. Right where he didn't want to be.

Terrific.

CHAPTER NINETEEN

Forget borrowed time. Los Angeles lives on borrowed water.

As long as the city has been there, it has had a water problem. Los Angeles is next to the Pacific Ocean, but ocean water is not drinkable. Desalination is still expensive and imperfect.

And while it's hard to tell, looking at the golf courses, the mile after mile of houses with grass yards and palm trees and commercial buildings and used-car lots where men go outside every morning to hose the accumulated smog and grit off the cars, Los Angeles is a desert.

The city has to buy its water.

They had tried stealing it. They took water from the Owens Valley, in central California, beginning in the 1920s. The theory was that no one lived there anyway, so no one would miss it.

But people did live there. People farmed the Owens Valley, or tried to. Birds used Mono Lake as part of the Pacific Flyway, a stopover on their way north or south in the winter and summer.

Los Angeles drained the lake, and only recently was forced to stop.

Then there is the Colorado River, which runs through several western states on its way to the Gulf of Mexico. At least, it used to reach the Gulf of Mexico. Now, such demands have been made on its water that it peters out before it actually reaches the Gulf, slowing to a trickle and then drying up somewhere in Baja California, Mexico.

Los Angeles will take water wherever it can be found. With so many people, water is a resource more precious than gold. The average person in Los Angeles uses 130 gallons a day. And that doesn't count the people hosing off cars.

And all of it has to be treated before it enters the municipal water system. The Department of Water and Power runs a state-of-the-art treatment plant in the foothills of the San Gabriel Mountains, just north of the city. There, a combination of ozonation, filtration, and chlorination is applied to create drinking water that meets or exceeds all state and federal standards for cleanliness and health. The San Gabriel plant can treat 600 million gallons of water a day.

Harold Wechsler stood on the crest of the dam overlooking the reservoir. It was filled almost to capacity with water that would soon be put through the appropriate paces and sent out into the city through a complex system of water mains and pipes. There was a narrow roadway across the dam crest, with a walkway next to it. Wechsler was on the walkway, leaning against the low retaining wall, looking down the vast slope of concrete that led to the water. At the bottom of the wall, the water was fed into the sophisticated filtration systems. It churned there like a monstrous washing machine, and the roar of it was thunderous up here. It smelled rank, unclean, on this side. When it came out, it was fresh and pure.

Barry Fetzer squatted nearby pulling items from a canvas gym bag. "Here's the scroll, Hal," he shouted. He held out the ancient rolled sheet. Wechsler took it and unrolled it, holding it by the gold bars at its top and bottom.

The scroll was thousands of years old, hand-painted on a thin, leathery sheet of something yellow. People had claimed that the yellow material was human skin, but Wechsler didn't think so. The texture wasn't quite right for that. But there were several types of demons whose skin it could have been, and he was sure it could easily be one of them.

The words were painted on the scroll by hand, in

letters about half an inch tall. The artist had illuminated the first letter, making it about three times the size of the others and surrounded with designs and curlicues. There were more designs down the sides and across the top of the scroll. In the bottom center was an eerily realistic depiction of a skull—not a human one—with three horns arrayed across its head and a snake's long body slithering out one of the eye sockets.

The skull had taken on, for Wechsler, the kind of comfortable familiarity some people felt about illustrations in their favorite children's books. But Wechsler, as a child, had never had books, or had access to them. His parents hadn't believed in reading to their only child. So he didn't have memories of the Cat in the Hat or the Wild Things or the Tawny Scrawny Lion. Instead, his earliest memories were of beatings and of scared, hushed conversations in which his parents worried that their secret might be compromised, that their true nature might be found out.

Wechsler, at this moment in his life, reveled in his true nature. Standing on the top of the dam, he put the scroll on the ground and took one more look around him—at the water twinkling in the last rays of moonlight, at Fetzer, looking on expectantly—and stripped his clothes off. His human clothes. As he did so, he allowed his demonic self to take over.

His skin darkened, becoming a kind of eggplant purple. He began to grow a tail, which stopped when it was a thick appendage nearly two feet long with a spiked ball at the end of it. His fingers grew also, thickening and splaying out, with webbing between them and long, sharp claws at the ends. His chest deepened, his shoulders grew broader, his muscles more developed.

As a human, he was not especially weak but neither was he particularly strong. As a demon, though, he was massive and powerful. The strength he hadn't known as a young man had come to him later in life. It was glorious.

He ran a hand across his head, knobbed and heavily plated to protect his eyes and vitals. He opened his mouth, touched the ends of impressive fangs with a tongue that was practically prehensile.

When he spoke, even his voice was different, as raw and gravelly as that of a blues singer lost to booze and cigarettes. "Is that everything?" he asked Fetzer.

"That's it, Hal," Barry yelled over the roar of the water. "Everything you brought."

Wechsler cast an appraising glance at the array of items Barry had spread on the low wall. Four different powders, each brightly colored, almost fluorescent: tangerine, magenta, cyan, emerald. A glass jar containing the eyeballs of various creatures—not just newts, as in the stories, although he was sure that a couple of newts were represented. The eyes symbolized clarity, of thought and of purpose. A small filigreed box, closed, contained the heart of a bird. It was a tiny thing, but it symbolized freedom denied, flight tethered—opportunity squandered, in other words.

And the scroll, still on the ground at Wechsler's feet. He had read it so many times it was burned into his memory. But that didn't matter—when the time came, he still needed to read from the scroll itself. It wasn't just the words; it was the act of reading from the scroll that held magical significance. In magic, there was nothing arbitrary, nothing random. Everything needed to be done the right way or there was no purpose to doing it at all. Jules Lefler had taught him that. Experience had borne it out.

Wechsler allowed himself a moment to reflect before he began the ceremony. He remembered the path that had brought him here. The unhappy childhood that had stretched into the teen years, the victim mentality, the petty crimes. Then the discovery of Lefler's book and the beginning of his rise to power. Years in the streets, doing whatever it took to get by. And then he had begun to amass wealth and to attract still more wealth. Connections had come with that. Then power, germinating like a seed, sprouting, reaching out in a hundred different directions at once as it fed on itself. Where once he had been unable to afford a car, he ultimately reached the point where he was driven around in limousines, which he owned. The young man who couldn't get a date had beautiful women throwing themselves at him. The loser who wasn't taken seriously by the big guys on the corner was handed the top job in the nation's largest municipally owned utility because he had helped the mayor get elected.

And while even the mayor didn't know it, Wechsler's current job was the one he had had his eye on since the 1960s. Because this was the job that would open the right doors. Who else could drive up to the gates of the city's main water treatment plant at four in the morning and be allowed in without the slightest hesitation or question? Who else would be permitted to walk alone out onto the dam crest, after posting his own guards near the gates to ensure that he would not be disturbed? No one. The president of the United States could not have pulled this off.

But the general manager of the DWP could.

Wechsler lifted the scroll, unrolled it again, and began to read.

Barry Fetzer knew his part, as assistant. Wechsler had walked him through it, time and again. When Wechsler nodded, Barry would pour. Wechsler had no doubt of that.

If he failed, he would end up in the water too. And he wouldn't be coming out.

"Ia! Ia!" Wechsler began. His voice was soft at

first, but then grew louder, as he was caught up in reading these passages aloud for the first time in his life. *"Gog sutthok olt slivgen ud brialt! Ia! Ia! Wisler friou kakaroth!"*

He inclined his head toward the colored powders. Barry uncapped the cyan and emptied it over the water, holding it at arm's length as he did. The wind picked up the trail of powder and whisked it out over the reservoir, a metallic blue contrail in the moonlight that disappeared over the dark expanse of water.

It was begun.

Angel braked the Plymouth to a stop outside the front gates of the San Gabriel treatment plant. There was a guardhouse next to the gate, but no one came out of it to greet them. Angel climbed out of the car, and Slade followed. Angel tugged at the gates.

"Locked."

Slade drew his .38 and pointed it at the gates.

"That won't help," Angel told him. "They're electronic. You can't just shoot the lock. Anyway, a gate isn't likely to believe in you."

"Guess that's true."

"I have a real gun, if it'll help," Barbara said.

Angel shook his head and grabbed one gate in each hand, standing at the center between them, and pulled.

Nothing.

He tried again. The muscles in his arms and back stood up, bunched and taut beneath his shirt and coat. Veins popped on his neck with the effort. He spread his legs for leverage and tugged with everything he had.

And the gates began to open.

He kept pulling, but it got easier once they had started. The electronic locking mechanism was meant to hold them together, and once that point was passed, they just swung open.

Angel tossed a quick smile to the others. "Let's go," he said.

"Um, Angel," Cordelia said hesitantly. "Friends of yours?"

Angel spun back around. Coming down the roadway toward the gates were three demons. *At least they're carrying my kind of weapons*, Angel thought. One had a battle-ax with a head at least three feet across, on a six-foot pole. Another demon had a heavy mace with nine-inch spikes in the ball end. The third carried a double-handed broadsword, both edges sharpened.

The demons themselves were seven feet tall, and broad-shouldered. Their faces were barely recognizable as such, mostly hidden behind long fleshy tendrils. They wore dark strips of fabric wrapped around them haphazardly like rags.

Angel let the transformation wash over him, and braced himself for a fight.

Barbara stepped out of the guardhouse. "Authorized visitors came in forty minutes ago, according to the log. No red flag, so they were okay. There're two guards inside," she announced. "At least, two heads. I didn't count the other pieces."

A hard fight, Angel thought.

"Yuck," Cordelia said. "But, you're good."

"What do you mean?" Barbara asked her.

"I mean, if I had gone in there, the first and last thing I would have noticed would have been the body parts. Once I realized there were parts, I wouldn't have hung around to find out anything else."

"She's right," Slade said. "You'll be a good cop yet, ponytail."

Angel stopped listening to the chatter behind him. The demons were closing in. Suddenly Slade stepped up beside Angel, his Browning in his fist.

"They may not believe in me either," he said. "But then again, a ghost gun might be just as good against freak shows like these as anything else we could throw at 'em."

"You could be right," Angel said. Then there was movement on his other side, and he saw Barbara, service revolver in her hands, taking up a firing position.

"I'll just, umm, stay back here and make sure the car's safe," Cordelia called from behind Angel.

"That's fine, Cord," he replied. "That's where I want you."

"Do we shoot them?" Barbara asked.

"They ain't the Welcome Wagon," Slade told her.

The demons took another couple of steps toward them.

"Now?" Barbara asked.

"Now," Slade answered. Both of them started to fire. Their shots were loud in the rural stillness, competing only with the distant rush of water. The acrid tang of gun smoke stung Angel's nostrils.

The bullets found their marks.

The demons jerked as they were hit. They snarled, a sound not unlike that of a dog defending its food.

But they didn't fall. They shook off the impacts and kept coming.

"This is what I was afraid of," Angel said.

"Shoot for the brain," Slade instructed. "If they got brains."

"If they have brains, they might just as easily be in their feet," Angel said. "Unless you know something about their physiology that I don't."

Slade and Barbara fired again anyway. Once again the demons paused, worked through any pain they might have felt, and continued their steady approach. The weapons moved in their hands, and as they grew nearer, they spread out and began to swing them in slow, widening arcs.

"You'd better let me deal with them," Angel said. He moved ahead of the others.

Angel would ordinarily have started with whichever one looked like the greatest threat, but in this case they all looked pretty intimidating. Since the mace wielder was in the middle, he started there.

He charged that one. The demon drew back the mace and then swung it like a baseball bat, starting out low and rising through the arc. Angel ducked below it, and the demon's momentum wouldn't allow him to stop it until it had followed through the arc. By that time, Angel was in close. The thing's fetid breath was in his face. It smelled like Angel imagined a fish market, closed for five years with its inventory in place but no cooling facilities, might smell. He ignored it and attacked.

He threw two right jabs into the thing's midsection, then a left hook up into the mass of tendrils that was its face. Some of the tendrils looped around his wrist and held it. He couldn't yank it free. He reared back and kicked the creature in the middle with his right foot, then dropped, sprang up again, and followed with his left.

The demon took a step back under the onslaught, and Angel was able to jerk his wrist free.

"Keep away from those viney things!" Slade called out to him.

I figured that out, Angel thought.

As the thing started to regain its balance, it drew the mace back for another swing. Angel was still in close, though he hadn't been able to figure out how to actually damage the demon. The other demons had gone past him; from the corner of his eye he could see the sword wielder getting closer to Barbara and Slade.

He had to finish this fast.

So he went for the mace.

One thing Angel understood about demons: if they carried weapons, there was a reason for it. Demons this size could take humans apart like a child with a rag doll, if they wanted. The guards at the gate had apparently learned this. So the fact that they carried weapons was indicative not only of their strengths but of their weaknesses as well.

He feinted left and then dodged to the right, getting back behind the huge demon. The thing was just starting to bring the mace around, but it hadn't yet gained any momentum. Angel grabbed the demon's wrists and stopped the swing.

The demon cranked its head around and regarded him, its small black eyes looking at him questioningly.

Angel brought his knee up under the thing's wrists and snapped them.

The demon let out a long howl, the first sound they'd heard any of the demons make. Its mouth was a black pit that opened among the tendrils.

It dropped the mace.

Angel shoved the demon, and it fell away a couple of steps, weak from the pain of having its arms broken. Angel scooped up the mace, which was surprisingly heavy. He swung it, as the demon had, coming from low to high, baseball style.

The spiked head of the mace slammed into the demon's chest.

Several of the spikes buried themselves in the thing's flesh. The demon screamed again and fell over.

Now the other demons turned on Angel. They had been past him, headed toward Slade and Barbara Morris. But they'd identified Angel as the greater threat, he figured, because they were both coming at him, from opposite sides.

Maintaining some distance from each other.

Good strategy.

He'd been hoping for bad strategy.

The one with the sword reached him first. The sword whistled as its keen blade cut the air. Angel parried with the mace's handle.

From the other side, though, the battle-ax streaked toward him. Angel dodged.

Which put him closer to the sword demon, who was thrusting his weapon forward for a second strike.

Angel turned, presenting a smaller target, but still the blade cut the flesh over the ribs.

He gritted his teeth, swung the mace.

The demon parried with the sword. Took a step back. Feinted once, twice. Thrust again.

And when Angel dodged it, the battle-ax came sailing toward him.

Angel dropped, flattening himself on the ground. Just above him, the battle-ax slammed into the sword blade.

The blade shattered. Shards of steel rained down around Angel. He covered his head with his hands, having let go of the mace as soon as he hit the ground. Steel bounced off the roadway around him.

The sword demon grunted furiously at the battle-ax demon. The battle-ax wielder's body language was defensive, ax drawn back, head thrust out.

They were arguing.

Angel grabbed up the mace and pushed himself to his feet, bringing the mace up at the same time.

The battle-ax demon was gesticulating with its chin as it sputtered at the demon whose sword had broken.

The mace caught that chin, and continued up.

The demon's head snapped back, tore at the neck.

A gout of blood jetted into the night sky.

Angel didn't hang around to watch the demon fall. As soon as he knew it was dead he started a new swing, at the sword demon. The thing tried to parry with the stub of a blade left in its fist, but it couldn't stop the great mace.

A moment later, Angel took a deep breath. Three bodies littered the road, and he was wet and sticky with their blood.

And some of his own, he remembered. The cut over his ribs hurt. He wondered if the demons' weapons were enchanted.

If they were just steel, his wound would heal quickly. If they were silver, it would take longer.

If they were magical, it might never heal. It might be the wound that would finally kill him.

But if he didn't stop Wechsler, it wouldn't matter if he lived or died: it would be too late for everyone.

"Let's go," Angel said.

While I still can.

CHAPTER TWENTY

They ran up the hill away from the front gate. Barbara and Slade both had guns in their hands, in case they ran into anything that could be effectively shot at. Angel breathed through his teeth, willing the pain away. Cordelia came behind them, clutching a crossbow Angel had pulled from the trunk for her.

At the top of this first hill there was a big, low building—the control center for the treatment plant, Angel assumed. The road continued on past that structure, though, swooping downhill toward a vast reservoir. He could barely make out the water, a dark patch against the dark hills, but here and there it sparkled with a reflection of the sinking moon or the last stars.

Another problem, Angel thought. If this took too

long, the sun would come up, and then it wouldn't matter if he was wounded or not.

At the near end of the big reservoir, there was a wall. Water went into the wall on the far side and apparently came out through big pipes on this side, on its way into the treatment system.

As soon as they topped the rise they could hear and smell the water, much louder than it was down by the gates. The water rumbled like a nonstop thunderclap.

But over the water, when the wind was right, Angel could hear something else. Then he saw them, on the wall—a tall, dark demon and a man. The demon held something in its hands and was screeching at the water in some unknown tongue.

Angel didn't recognize it, but he assumed it was Melechian.

The demon was Wechsler. And he was reading from the scroll.

Angel didn't hesitate. He kept running, past the control buildings toward the dam. The others tried to keep up with him. Only Slade came close.

"Where are you going?" Cordelia asked Barbara. "Angel's going that way!"

"You can stay with him if you want," Barbara said. "Or you can stick with me. Just keep out of my way."

She had stopped at the big building on top of the hill. There was a sign next to the door: San Gabriel

Water Treatment Plant—Administration Building 102L. Barbara gave one glance at the rapidly disappearing Angel and Slade, and tried the door. It didn't budge.

That was when Cordelia made her decision. "I'll stick with you, I guess," Cordelia said. "You're more likely to need my help than Angel is."

"Never know," Barbara said. She tossed Cordelia a knowing grin. "You know that stuff about bashing down doors with your shoulder? That's TV. Much easier just to shoot your way in, if you don't have a battering ram."

She leveled her service revolver, aiming at the dead-bolt lock set into the heavy steel door. She squeezed the trigger twice.

Cordelia tucked the crossbow under her arm and put her hands over her ears after the first loud report, but it was too late—they were already ringing.

Barbara delivered a sharp, well-placed kick just below the lock. The door swung open.

"You learn that in the Academy?" Cordelia asked.

Barbara shook her head. "I learned it from Mom," she replied. "She said she learned it from Mike Slade."

They entered the building. Fluorescent lights gleamed from overhead fixtures in the hall, but the place felt empty.

"What are we doing in here?" Cordelia asked.

She didn't like this place, didn't like being away from Angel, didn't like not knowing what was going on.

"The way I figure it, we'll know the answer to that when we see it," Barbara replied. She led the way down the hall, revolver gripped in both hands the way Cordelia had seen on television.

I guess her mother didn't learn everything from Mike Slade, she thought. Slade always carried his gun in one meaty fist. The manly way.

"*Fothoris cren bisrilat!*" Wechsler chanted. He held the scroll high in front of him. At a nod of Wechsler's head, Barry emptied the jar of eyes into the churning, roiling water and put the jar back into the gym bag. Only the small box was left on the wall.

Wechsler was hyperaware: he could taste the water, could see every individual droplet of it, could hear it whispering to him over the furious roar.

So when someone stepped onto the road at the end of the dam crest, he knew it.

And he knew who it was.

Slade.

But he couldn't stop now. He was almost to the end of the scroll—and, once begun, the ritual had to be performed through to the end.

He kept reading.

"*Bobispat snarleth krre greong,*" he intoned.

"Wechsler!" Slade shouted, his voice barely carrying over the water's din.

"*Gog visitoth magog bylend,*" he continued, ignoring Slade. "*Cunow shilleptor saffold. Ia! Ia!*"

He nodded his head. Barry, watching for the cue, opened the small box and shook the bird's heart out. It tumbled into the darkness below, out of sight almost instantly. Its splash, in the overall roar, was imperceptible.

Done.

Wechsler rolled up the scroll and turned to face his visitors.

Slade was not alone. With him was a tall man, strong-looking, with dark clothes and spiky brown hair. As he drew closer, Wechsler amended his thought. Not a man at all. A vampire.

Stranger and stranger, he thought.

A ghost and a vampire, confronting me on the most significant night of my life.

And for nothing. Wasting their time, and mine.

He smiled.

Angel didn't like that smile at all.

It was too self-congratulatory for his taste. Smug, even. His first close-up look at Harold Wechsler, and he already disliked him.

Of course, the Wechsler standing before them looked very little like the one he'd seen in the distance, inside his house. That one had looked human; this one was clearly a demon—purple-skinned with a stout tail that looked like a weapon and with horn-like knobs on his head. The facial features were vaguely recognizable, though.

"If you were trying to stop me," Wechsler said, the human voice barely understandable coming from the demonic mouth, "you're a little late."

"Never too late to put you away," Slade snarled. He held his gun at his waist, waving the barrel between Wechsler and his stooge. The smaller man was frozen in terror.

"Ah, but you're wrong," Wechsler retorted. "You can put me in any prison on earth. I won't even spend the night there."

"You're pretty sure of yourself," Angel said.

"I have every right to be."

"Maybe so," Angel replied. "And then, maybe not."

"What's he talkin' about, Angel?" Slade asked, confused. "What's he done?"

"I'm sure he'll correct me if I'm wrong," Angel told him. "But this is what I think, based on as much of the scroll as I was able to read. Wechsler hooked all those demons on Flux way back in your time, right?"

"That's right," Slade replied. Wechsler looked on with some interest, as if anxious to hear his story recited by someone else.

"The drugs made them appear to be human, and

killed them, right? That's how you told it to me."

"Yeah," Slade agreed.

"Except that it didn't really kill them," Angel continued. "Not the way you and I understand death. They're dead, for all intents and purposes. But not so dead that they can't come back."

"Come back?"

"That's right. The scroll describes a reanimation spell. And something about the water here—I think Wechsler has altered the water in some way so that it will act as the reanimation agent. When it hits the graves of all those supposedly dead demons, they'll return to some kind of life." Angel turned to Wechsler. "Is that about right?"

"Very good," Wechsler said. "You're only forgetting one very significant point."

"Right," Angel said, nodding his head. "When the demons come back, they'll belong to Weschler. They'll be under his complete control."

"And we're talking about hundreds of demons?" Slade inquired.

"Thousands," Wechsler said. "I never take half measures. Thousands of demons, mine to command. Demons have never been able to work together effectively. If they had, they would own the world. But they will cooperate now, because they will all take orders from me."

"That's good to know," Slade growled, "because it gives me one more reason to see you dead!"

He charged at Wechsler, but Wechsler stood his ground. As Slade came close, Wechsler swiveled his hips and his spike-ended tail whipped around, catching Slade in the stomach. The ghost detective reeled back, clutching at himself.

"Unnh!" he cried. "That hurt. Didn't know I could still be hurt."

"I'm the one who put you down to begin with," Wechsler reminded him. "And cast a spell over your remains. I have more power over you than you know."

Slade straightened up. "Maybe," he agreed. "But that won't stop me from killing you."

"Slade," Angel started. "Maybe—"

But Slade aimed his Browning and fired seven times, at point-blank range, into Wechsler's head.

Wechsler simply ignored the shots. They had no impact on him.

Slade threw the gun at Wechsler. It bounced off.

"Let me," Angel said.

Slade snarled at him. "He's mine."

He hurled himself at Wechsler again. This time he landed with enough force to drive Wechsler back a couple of steps. Slade pressed the attack, driving his fists into Wechsler's torso again and again, jackhammering him. He was in too close for Wechsler to use his tail, but he tore at Slade with his claws, snapped at him with big teeth.

Slade ignored the pain.

Slade pounded Wechsler, driving him back and back. Wechsler howled, an animal sound. Spittle strung between his teeth, escaped his mouth. His fists rained on Slade's back and head, but the detective was in another space, oblivious to the injuries being done to him.

Barry Fetzer started to run. Angel let him go. He wasn't the problem here, and if Slade fell to Wechsler, Angel would have to step in.

Wechsler jabbed a thumb toward Slade's eye. Slade dodged it, butted Wechsler in the chin with his head. Then he pushed off with his feet, reached up, and threw his arms around Wechsler's neck.

He squeezed and twisted.

Wechsler let out another howl of rage and pain.

Slade was trying to break the demon's neck. It looked to Angel as if he might succeed.

Angel heard a snapping sound.

Wechsler went limp.

Slade relaxed his grip.

That was when Wechsler let out a furious, unintelligible roar and brought both fists down on Slade's head, smashing the detective to the ground.

Wechsler began to kick him and bash him with his spiked tail.

Slade moaned.

Angel moved in.

Slade waved him away. "He's mine," he said again. Angel could barely understand him. His face was torn and bloody. His jaw didn't move right, and Angel realized it was broken. One arm was canted at an unnatural angle, also broken.

"Slade," Angel began.

"Mine," Slade repeated.

Wechsler kept up the assault, pounding Slade with blow after blow.

Slade mustered strength from somewhere and lashed out with his feet. He caught Wechsler's legs in a scissors grip and twisted. Wechsler went down in a heap.

Slade, broken and bleeding, forced himself to his feet.

He piled into Wechsler again, fists flying, feet flailing. Wechsler took hit after hit.

Slade doubled his fists together, drew back, and swung his arms like a club, slamming his fists into Wechsler's head. The demon's head snapped back, hard.

Slade had already injured Wechsler's neck. This blow finished it.

Wechsler screamed, agony and outrage and frustration combining in his inhuman throat to make a sound that was painful to hear. He reached for his head with both hands. He stumbled.

The low retaining wall was right behind him.

He backed into it. At seven feet tall, his legs were too long, his center of gravity too high.

He went over.

Angel and Slade both rushed to the wall. They caught a glimpse of Wechsler bouncing down the concrete slope, and then he was gone in the dark and the mist of the churning water below. His scream was lost in the water's ferocious thunder.

Slade, unable to maintain his balance, started to fall. Angel caught the detective, held him in his arms. "It's okay," he said, trying to sound calm. "Wechsler's gone. It's over."

"No, it's not," Slade spat through broken teeth. Blood ran from his nose and mouth. "Far from it."

CHAPTER TWENTY-ONE

Doyle was back inside the cemetery. He had picked a spot on a grassy slope overlooking Betty McCoy's grave. So as not to present a silhouette to any security guards who might be roaming about, he was sitting down, even though the grass was damp with the night dew. Sitting with his back to the bank, anyone would have to come right up on him with a light to see him here.

It will be just another hour or so until the sun comes up, he thought. Then he could get out of here. He hoped the others were having as quiet a night as he was. He hated to think that maybe they were in some kind of trouble or danger while all he could do was sit here and watch a quiet grave.

Well, he reflected, *I don't hate the part where I'm not in danger.* But he liked Angel and Cordy, and he didn't want them in danger either.

Still, if there was anything going on, he decided, *I'd have heard about it when I talked to Angel.*

He heard a sound and pressed himself deeper into the wet grass.

It was kind of a *thunk*. There was, with it, some sort of movement, but at first he couldn't make it out.

He listened, and tried to peer through the darkness to see what it was. It was somehow familiar, and yet it filled him with dread.

Then another sound, more of a *tchhh-thunk*, followed by a *chk-chk-chk-chk-chk*.

And water splashed over him.

Sprinklers!

Just what he needed.

Angel had told him to stay put until sunrise.

But the sprinklers were timed to work before sunrise. Made sense in southern California. Lawns were watered before the sun was up, if possible, because the sunlight beaming through water droplets would be magnified. The sun on freshly watered grass could actually burn the blades just like a kid burning holes in leaves by angling the sun through a magnifying glass. Better to water before the sun came up, so the water could soak into the ground before the day grew hot.

Doyle understood the theory. But that didn't mean he wasn't getting wet.

Every time the rotating sprinkler *chk-chk-chk*ed

its way back to him, he got soaked. He'd be drenched to the bone in no time.

But did he abandon his post again? Or stay here and take it?

What harm could a little water do? he wondered. He lay back on the grass and decided to stay.

Barbara and Cordy moved through the seemingly deserted building, opening doors more or less at random as they passed down the hall.

On the first floor they found no one.

Ditto the second floor.

But there was a basement.

They took the stairs three at a time, Barbara in front, her ponytail flopping as she descended.

Downstairs they found people.

Barbara tried one of the doors. She read the little plastic sign next to it: Control. That seemed to be a good place to look. The knob was locked. She pounded on the door with her fist. "LAPD!" she shouted. "Open up!"

"What happened to just shooting the lock?" Cordelia asked.

"If there're people inside and you might want their cooperation, it's sometimes better to talk first, shoot later," Barbara explained.

No one came to the door.

Barbara pounded again.

"Police!" she called.

"Can you prove it?" someone from inside asked, voice tentative.

There was no peephole, and the door was too tight to shove anything underneath.

"I can show you my shield, but you'll have to open the door to see it," she said. "This is a police emergency. Please open the door."

"There was shooting," the voice from inside said. It was a male voice, a little high pitched.

That could have been from tension, Cordelia realized. She wouldn't blame anyone inside for being a little nervous, considering that someone had shot their way into the building in the middle of the night.

"We were not shooting at people, just at the lock," she said. "People-shooting is definitely not on our to-do list."

Barbara glared at her. Cordelia shrugged. "Just trying to help," she said. "I'm big on people skills."

"Let me do the talking," Barbara hissed. She turned back to the door. "Please, sir, just open the door. You know I can shoot my way in if I have to. I'd rather not have to do that. There's no need to alarm anyone inside, but this is a police emergency and I'm asking for your cooperation."

The door clicked and the knob turned. A small man opened it partway. He had thinning reddish hair and thick glasses over bright blue eyes. He wore a white shirt with a narrow dark tie, and a plastic pocket protector held pens.

Barbara held a leather case up in front of his face. "Here's my identification," she said. He looked at it, eyes wide and unblinking. His gaze traveled to the crossbow that Cordelia carried, then back to the I.D.

"I'm still in the Academy; I'm not a full-fledged police officer yet," Barbara told him. "But I'm here on a case, and as I said, this is an emergency. Please open the door all the way."

"O-okay," the little man said. He complied.

"What's your name?" Barbara asked him.

"Daly," the man said. "John Daly."

"Is there anyone else inside, Mr. Daly?"

"Yes, there are three of us. George Coxe and Freddie Nebel."

"We're coming in," Barbara informed him. She and Cordelia entered the room.

Just inside was kind of an anteroom. There was a desk with a computer monitor and keyboard on it, and beyond that there was another doorway.

"Where are they?" Barbara wanted to know.

"They're in there," Daly said, pointing toward the other door. "This is Water Central. We run things from here."

"Perfect," Barbara said. "Let's go."

Doyle was resigned to getting wet. Every thirty seconds or so, the sprinkler came back around to spray him. He had decided that it wasn't so bad—he was cold, but that would pass. And he'd been cold during the night anyway, and the dew had already made his back wet, so getting wetter and colder wasn't really that big a deal. He almost dozed off, dreaming of hot coffee before a roaring fireplace.

But that was before the wet earth started to move.

From his place on the slope, he could see about two dozen graves besides Betty McCoy's. Some of the headstones bore the names of demon families; others didn't. From here he couldn't read any of the names.

So when the grass over one of the graves started to shift, he wasn't instantly sure whether the grave belonged to one of the demons or not.

Either way, he didn't like it.

Grass was supposed to stay put. It wasn't supposed to undulate like that.

And then a hand shot out from it.

Not a human hand. Doyle could see that right off, even in the dim light. It was much too big and squared off to be human. The fingers were gnarled and bent, but the overall shape and size of the hand reminded him of a tray from a toaster oven, only thicker, pushing up through the ground from below.

Followed, almost immediately, by the rest of the arm.

It flailed about for a moment, then flattened itself against the grass, clutching and straining as if someone were trying to pull himself up from below.

Which *was exactly what seemed to be happening*.

He had to fight down the momentary urge to lend a hand, as if someone were drowning in his presence.

But this wasn't a matter of saving the life of some innocent. This was a demon, buried in the ground, trying to get out.

There was something definitely not good going on in the graveyard. All Doyle really wanted to do was run.

But he was supposed to watch Betty McCoy's grave. And if something bad was happening, it could also happen to her.

He had to stay.

He hated to stay.

But orders were orders. And so far, Angel hadn't asked him to do anything that was wrong, strictly speaking. He had asked Doyle to do things that were dangerous. Doyle frowned on that, but he knew the drill. Both of them, really, were working for the same things—for the Powers That Be, for justice in an unjust world, for the benefit of people in need.

Their kind had done plenty of harm to humans. Doyle and Angel were just trying to pay them back a little.

Doyle kept telling himself that as he watched the demon emerge from the grave.

He was expecting to see a moldering, decomposed demon corpse. But this demon looked as fresh as if he had gone into the ground yesterday. As his head cleared the earth, he shook it, knocking off some of the dirt that had fallen in on him. Doyle could see green spots on scaly pinkish skin, and a tuft of shocking pink hair. A Bejreggan demon, then. They didn't look dangerous, but looks were often deceiving—and in this case they definitely were. Bejreggans were brutal, nasty creatures. This one was part of the Parsons family, according to the gravestone, he remembered. And the Parsons family had blended pretty well into human society. But Bejreggans who had not blended were some of the most violent, vicious demons in the city.

Doyle hoped this one didn't see him. He couldn't imagine what kind of mood a Bejreggan might be in after clawing his way up from the grave. But he suspected that "not cheerful" didn't even begin to cover it.

He was so focused on the Bejreggan, in fact, that he almost didn't hear the two demons walking up behind him until they were on top of him.

A cracking twig caught his attention, and he spun around. Two more demons were right behind him, dirt still caking their hair and faces and burial garb, streaked from the sprinkler water. They started to walk past, but one of them was slowly swiveling his head from side to side as he walked, and he spotted Doyle on the end of his swivel.

"Look," he said. His voice was slow and deep,

almost as if he were talking in slow motion. The demon next to him, a female, turned to see what he was pointing at.

Doyle pushed himself to his feet, ready to run or fight.

Both demons turned toward him, and then behind him the Bejreggan gave a little grunt and started up the hill toward him from that side.

Standing now, Doyle could see more graves than before. And he could see more demons shoving themselves up out of those graves. All around, there were collapsed graves, imploded grass and dirt, where someone had come up from beneath. And all around, there were demons, shambling, still moving slowly as if they had just awakened from a long sleep and hadn't quite gotten their bearings.

And they were mostly looking at him.

"Hey, I'm a demon too," Doyle said. He allowed his human side to fade and his demon colors to show through. But even as the inch-long blue spikes extruded from his skin, he knew that it wasn't his humanity they were locking on to so much as it was the realization that he was not fresh from the grave. It was as if they held a grudge against him because he hadn't died and come back.

At least that was how it looked from Doyle's vantage point.

And if he was right, he was in trouble. They surrounded him, they more than outnumbered him.

Doyle turned in a slow circle, trying to keep them all in sight. But they were coming from every side now. They had started talking, their voices low and quiet. The sound was a distant rumble, like traffic on the other side of a wall. He couldn't make out the words, only the noise.

And the sense that it wasn't friendly.

"Now I'm one of you," he said. "Nothin' to say we can't be best buds, eh? Let's talk this over."

Which was when the Bejreggan grabbed him.

The control room looked like Houston Mission Control to Cordelia. There was an enormous screen on one wall, but instead of showing astronauts in space or a rocket on a launching pad, it was a gigantic illuminated diagram, in bright colors, that meant absolutely nothing to her. She supposed it showed, in some format, the delivery system for the city's water supply. But she didn't understand any of it.

In front of that were banks of computers, some of which had the same diagram on their monitors and some of which had columns of numbers or words. She didn't get close enough to try to make sense of those.

Daly had brought them inside, at Barbara's insistence, and introduced them to Coxe and Nebel. Coxe was a male engineer, basically indistinguishable from Daly, Cordelia thought, except that his stomach was bigger and his tie carried the stains of dozens of meals, most of which seemed to have included taco sauce. Freddie Nebel was a woman—in her mid-thirties, Cordelia guessed—who was basically the female equivalent of the two men. Overall, Cordelia figured that the people who ran water treatment plants might be very nice, but they weren't the kind of people she'd have chosen to hang out with in her free time.

On the other hand, she realized, none of them had asked her out or really given her much more than a glance, so maybe they were thinking the same thing about her.

That was hard to believe, but within the bounds of remote possibility.

They were charged with keeping the plant running overnight, Daly explained. There was a much larger staff on during the day, including all the administrators and business people. But at night little happened. They continued to run water through the filtration and ozonation processes, because the city's demand for water never stopped. But that was all. It was mostly routine, and three of them could do it.

"How hard is it to stop the water?" Barbara asked.

Daly blinked a couple of times, an action that was magnified dramatically by the thickness of his glasses. "What do you mean?" he asked.

"Stop the water. Shut it down. Turn it off."

"Turn off the filters?"

"Turn off the water completely. Stop letting it into the city."

"That's impossible!" Freddie interjected.

"Literally impossible?"

"No, she doesn't mean that," Daly interjected. It was almost as if, having invited them in, he had made them his guests and would take their side over that of his colleagues. "It's not easy, but we can do it. I think Freddie means it isn't within the scope of our duties."

"Well, of course," Freddie said, speaking for herself. "To shut the plant down we'd have to have orders from the DWP. And that's not something that they would undertake lightly. You're talking about separating three and a half million people from their water supply. The uproar would be incredible."

"So if I told you to do it right now . . ."

"We'd tell you to go through channels, come back with the right paperwork, and we'll see you in two weeks," Freddie finished.

"I don't have two weeks," Barbara said. "I need it shut down right now. Immediately."

"As in this instant," Cordelia added. "She's a police officer, so you have to listen to her." She turned to Barbara and whispered, "Why?"

"I don't know," Barbara replied, also in a whisper. "I don't know what Wechsler is doing here, or what's going on outside. But knowing what we know about Wechsler pushing drugs and all, I figure if he's here in the middle of the night, then he's up to no good. He's probably tampering with the water supply. So I want it turned off. Once we find out what he's doing here we can turn it back on." She faced the engineers again. "Well?"

"Or what? You'll give us a ticket?" Freddie Nebel asked.

"I'm asking you, as a citizen, to cooperate with a law enforcement officer," Barbara told her. "If you refuse I'll place you under arrest and then tell you to do it. If you still refuse, I'll figure out how to do it myself. But then if I break anything, it will be on you."

Nebel, Coxe, and Daly looked at one another, worried expressions on their faces. "I say we should do it," Daly offered.

"Are you insane?" Nebel asked.

"She might start shooting again," Coxe said fearfully.

"I'm not going to shoot anyone," Barbara told them, then added, "unless I have to."

"I'll show you how it works," Daly volunteered.

"I don't care how it works," Barbara replied. "Just turn it off."

"All right. I'll turn it off," Daly agreed. "Come on, people. Let's help the police officer."

CHAPTER TWENTY-TWO

Angel floored the GTX, rocking Cordelia, Barbara Morris, and Mike Slade in their seats. The 210 south to the 10 east into downtown, then the 101 into Hollywood. As daylight grew closer, traffic started to get a little heavier on L.A.'s freeways, so he darted and weaved from lane to lane.

He was becoming the kind of driver he hated, Angel realized. But the urgency he felt was profound. Barbara had cleverly gone into the control building and had the water treatment plant shut down, so most of the water that Wechsler had performed his ritual over would stay right there in the reservoir until Angel could come up with a counterspell. Some of it had gone through the system, though. And he doubted that the process that turned river water into chlorinated drinking water had any cleansing effect on enchanted water.

So throughout the city, in any number of cemeteries, "dead" demons could be coming back to life if their graveyards' sprinkler systems had drawn on water that had been touched in any way by the water that Wechsler had enchanted.

Doyle and Betty McCoy were in one of those cemeteries. That was where Angel pointed the Plymouth's nose. That was why Angel gunned it.

He hoped they weren't too late.

Doyle let out a yelp when the Bejreggan's gnarled pink hands encircled his arm. He shook the arm free and spun around, lashing out with one hand in a karate chop. The Bejreggan took the chop with a chuckle of amusement. Doyle punched him, twice, in the face. The demon tried to raise his hands in self-defense, but he was still moving slowly, still shaking off the chilling effects of the grave, Doyle figured. The two blows had some effect—the thing went down on its knees, and Doyle followed with a kick that crashed into the Bejreggan's jaw, snapping his spine at the neck. The Bejreggan collapsed.

Hey, Doyle thought with a grin. *I might be able to beat these things after all. Slower'n molasses in Siberia, it looks like.*

The two who had come up behind him advanced toward him now. Behind them, Doyle could see at least a dozen more headed his way. They were still moving slowly, like extras from *Night of the Living Dead,* he thought. But there were a lot of them. Even slow, they could overwhelm him with numbers.

He had to get to work.

He chose the nearest one, the male, and leaped at him. The demon tried to put up his hands, but Doyle dodged them and got his arms around the demon's neck. He shoved it backward, hearing the satisfying snap that meant the spinal cord was severed, which was really the only way he could think of to stop demons who were already dead. Then he pushed the body of that one onto the female, and they both tumbled into the grass.

Doyle dodged another one and began to sprint for the exit. He'd come back with help. Or a shotgun. Or, even better, send help back with shotguns.

After running for a couple of minutes, he topped a rise, and the exit was in sight.

But so was the security guard, the one who had kicked him out earlier. The man was on his knees, tears running down his face. His gun was abandoned on the grass a few feet from him. He held his nightstick out to one side, as if he'd forgotten it was even in his hand.

Nine demons surrounded the man. Their circle was getting smaller by the second. The vague susurrus of their whispered words was loud, though still unintelligible.

The gate was two minutes away. Maybe less. In

just over a minute he could probably be outside the cemetery. And all the demons who might have interfered with his escape had turned their attention to the guard.

Oh, man, Doyle thought. *This really bites, don't it?*

He started to run again.

"You've driven better," Cordelia called from the back seat.

Angel ignored her. He'd pulled off the 101 and was headed down Sunset toward the cemetery. But he was paying little attention to the lane markings, including the double yellow line that was supposed to separate the eastbound traffic, which included the GTX, from the westbound, which did not.

Angel drove on the westbound side when he found it convenient.

Slade slouched in the passenger seat next to him. "Doll baby ain't kiddin'," he mumbled. "If I wasn't dead already, this ride would have finished me for sure."

Slade had taken some serious damage in the fight with Wechsler. His clothes were spattered with his own blood, and his face was bruised and broken. Angel figured the damage wasn't permanent, but Slade didn't seem to heal as fast as Angel did. The wound over his ribs from the demon's blade was already nearly gone.

Barbara and Cordelia rode in back. Angel was impressed that Barbara had managed to get the water turned off. The young lady would be a good cop one of these days. And that, he knew, was something the city definitely needed more of.

Although just now, considering his driving, Angel was glad there didn't seem to be any cops out on the streets.

Then the Hollywood Peaceful Rest Cemetery loomed on the left, and Angel made a sudden turn, tail swaying out a bit. He braked as he cranked the wheel, sending the GTX sliding up onto the sidewalk before the cemetery gates.

They jumped out. Angel threw himself into the gate, bursting it open. He paused just inside the graveyard for less than a second. Listened.

He ran toward the sounds of screaming.

Slade, Barbara, and Cordelia followed.

In a wide bowl-shaped area, Doyle and another man—a security guard, judging from the uniform—stood back to back. Ringing them were a couple of dozen demons, snarling and growling and vocalizing in a variety of demon tongues. They looked as if they had murder in mind.

The guard waved a nightstick ineffectually, as though he thought it was a torch whose fire would dissuade these demons. Doyle's hands were empty, and he had them balled into fists, waiting for one of the demons to make a move.

One did. This one was short, five feet tall at the most, but heavily muscled, with a broad back like that of a weight lifter, and four powerful arms that ended in big veiny hands. It swung at Doyle with one of the hands. Doyle dodged it and kicked back at the thing. Another hand whipped around and caught Doyle's leg, tugging on it, flipping him up in the air and slamming him down on his back. Even from here, Angel could hear the impact. He winced. Then he barreled down the hill at top speed.

When he reached the four-armed demon Angel unleashed a combination left-right-left kick, followed by two quick chops to either side of the thing's throat. It fell in a heap, its windpipe broken.

"Man, am I glad to see you," Doyle said as he struggled to his feet. "These guys just keep comin'. We been fightin' 'em off as best we could."

"Reinforcements are here," Angel said.

"It's like they just come up outta their graves for no reason," Doyle said, gasping for breath. "All over the boneyard."

"There's a reason."

"Figures. Don't tell me, 'cause I really don't think I wanna know."

"Doyle," Angel said.

"Yeah?"

"Shut up and fight."

They both shut up. And fought.

Slade and Barbara charged in after them, guns

blazing. Within a few minutes the immediate threat seemed to be gone. They all looked at each other, winded, a sea of demon corpses around them. But as the life vanished from them, so did their demonic aspect. The bodies in the grass looked fully human in death.

"Go back to your guardhouse," Angel told the guard, who was florid and winded. "We'll wrap up here."

The guard nodded and hustled away.

Doyle, Slade, and Barbara gathered around Angel, who gestured from one to the other by way of introduction. "Doyle," he said. "Mike Slade. Barbara Morris."

"Hey," Doyle said.

"Hey," Slade repeated.

"Nice work, there," Doyle went on, catching Slade's eye. "You're good."

"Thanks," Slade said.

Cordelia had remained up on the ridge, away from the fighting. She had left the crossbow behind but carried a short wooden spear carved to a sharp point. She called out, a nervous tremor in her voice. "Umm, guys? If you're all finished with the huddle down there, some more of those things are headed this way."

"Thanks, doll baby," Slade shouted.

"Like I said," Doyle offered, "they just keep comin'."

"There's got to be a finite number of them," Angel said.

"But it's a big number," Slade countered. "Wechsler was a busy guy. And a lot of the demon families used this graveyard. Not all of 'em, but plenty."

"This is where Betty McCoy's buried," Angel told him. "Doyle was keeping an eye on her grave."

"Until things started to go crazy, that is," Doyle said. Slade looked stunned. "Betty's here?"

At the same instant, they all realized what that could mean.

Doyle started to run toward her grave. "She's this way!" he called.

The rest of them ran with him. But Doyle knew where he was going, and he got there first.

The top of the grave had collapsed in on the emptiness inside. She was gone.

Doyle swiveled around looking in every direction. There were demons rambling around the grass, between tombstones, some almost to the fence. But he couldn't see any who looked like Betty McCoy.

On the other hand, he didn't know what she looked like. He had only seen the name and address in his vision, not the woman herself.

Angel caught up to him, standing beside the vacant grave. "Are we too late?" he asked.

"Too late," Doyle agreed.

*   *   *

Mike Slade had been through a lot in the past few days. Especially since, as far as his sense of time went, getting shot and killed had also happened in the last few days. Add to that being brought back to life, being chased all over the city by cops, meeting Veronica's daughter and finding out that his secretary and his last client were both dead.

Okay, he thought, time to stop kidding himself. Not just his secretary—the woman he had loved. The one tomato in a city full of 'em that made him think about settling down and getting married, buying a house in the suburbs, maybe giving up the racket and finding honest work.

With just a shake of her head or a swivel of her hip or a wink of one of those eyes, she could put thoughts like that into a guy's noggin. For years, he had told himself it was just that he had taken too many lumps there. But as time wore on, the thoughts didn't go away; instead they got worse and worse. Until the day that he confessed his feelings to her, fully expecting her to pack up her belongings and walk out the door. Instead, she had smiled at him, crossed her legs, and said, "Took you long enough, you big idiot."

But this wasn't the time to think about Veronica. The graveyard was full of reanimated demons, looking for direction and finding none because Slade had killed the guy who brought them back. They would just wander aimlessly, wreaking havoc, unless they were stopped.

And the only way to stop them was to kill them again. To incapacitate them, so their bodies couldn't carry out the instructions sent down by what was left of their brains.

This all rushed through Slade's head as he stood looking down at the place where Betty McCoy had lain, not restfully, these last years. He had found Wechsler and killed him. That should have been enough, he thought. But it wasn't, because, all these years later, he had been too late. He hadn't been able to prevent what Betty had wanted him to prevent, all those years before.

So Wechsler had won, and Slade had lost, because Betty's spirit still couldn't rest.

He scanned the grassy sward, watching the demons who sought freedom on the other side of the fence. The grass was no greener over there, he knew. There was no grass left in L.A. at all, except inside this fence. The city had changed, and not for the better. It was bigger and louder and dirtier and deadlier, but it had been a big, loud, dirty, dangerous place to begin with.

Then, almost to the fence, he saw her.

He'd have recognized her anywhere, anytime, he realized. The flip of her hair, the waggle of her hip and behind when she walked, the length of her neck. They didn't hire unattractive women to be cigarette girls, especially at a joint like the Rialto Lounge. A joint with ambitions of being more than a joint, of being a destination. And Betty was nothing if not attractive.

"Betty!" he yelled.

She didn't turn. But he knew it was her, even at this distance and in the gray hour before dawn.

Slade ran after her.

"Betty!"

He kept calling as he ran. Finally she heard him, stopped, turned.

There was no smile on her face. No flicker of recognition in her dead eyes.

Her hands opened and closed, as if seeking something to tear apart. Her lips were parted slightly, to reveal teeth that were caked with dirt from her grave.

"Betty," he said, pulling to a stop a couple of feet in front of her. "It's me, Mike. Mike Slade."

Still no sign that she knew him.

Or saw him as anything other than breakfast.

She licked her lips, streaking the dirt there.

Spittle showed on her tongue. Her mouth was literally watering.

She looked ravenous.

She lunged.

"Betty!" he shouted, pushing her away.

She didn't respond except to come at him again. This time, when he pushed her back, she latched on to his arm. Her fingernails dug into his flesh.

Her teeth snapped at his throat.

"I'm not what you want to eat," Slade said. "There's nothing here. I'd be like a Chinese meal, you'd be hungry again in an hour."

She didn't answer. She tore at him.

She meant to kill him.

It was the only thing these demons could do. The thing they'd been programmed for, by Harold Wechsler.

To kill and kill and kill.

"Betty, I'm sorry," Slade said, his voice catching. "I failed you. I should've killed him years ago, before he got me. I screwed up, honey. I blew it."

Betty snapped at him, her powerful arms drawing him ever closer to her jaws. Even in demon form, she looked mostly human. She was just preternaturally strong, and her normally straight white teeth were enlarged.

He knew he had only one choice. Not a choice at all, really.

The only thing he could do. The only way to give her any kind of peace.

He had to kill Betty McCoy.

Again.

Something clouded his vision, and he realized it was tears welling up in his eyes.

But private eyes never cried. Private eyes were the toughest guys in town. They could take anything. Emotions didn't get in their way. They were all about the case, the bad guy, the cash payment at the end of it.

Sometimes they were about justice. That guy, Angel, seemed to be about justice.

But also, private eyes were about doing what needed to be done.

Don't think about it, Slade told himself. *Don't worry about it, just do it.*

Slade did it.

When he was finished, he knelt in the grass with Betty McCoy in his arms, resting on his lap. The life, artificially restored as it was, ebbed out of her. Slade felt something too, a sense that he was disappearing again. He had only come back for Betty, he knew. To close this case, once and for all.

The case was closed. Wechsler was dead. Now Betty would be dead again and at rest.

He looked down at her even features, her milky skin, her surprisingly blue eyes.

And those eyes met his. And the lips pulled back in a smile.

"Mike," she said.

Her eyes closed.

She was gone.

Slade felt the tears again, and he couldn't stop them. They filled his eyes, rolled out onto his cheeks and down, down, splashing onto Betty's white skin.

"We'll take her, man," Doyle said.

Slade blinked. Doyle and Angel were there. They lifted Betty off him, gently carried her back toward her grave.

"I'm really glad you came back, Mike," Barbara said. She knelt in the wet grass beside him, stroking his shoulder with one hand.

"Me too, ponytail," he told her.

"It's like . . . it's like you're my dad, in a way. My real dad. My spiritual dad, I mean."

"I know. It's the same for me." He chuckled. "Only the other way around."

"I get it." She put her arms around him, pressed her face against his.

He could feel that her cheeks were also wet, but he couldn't really see her anymore. He couldn't see much of anything. The cemetery, Angel and Doyle and Cordelia and Betty—they were just hazy shapes, as if he was looking at them through several layers of gauze.

"I've changed my plans," Barbara continued. "I'll finish up at the Academy and do a stint on the force. But then I'm going to quit, go private. I think there are worse things than being a P.I."

"See if you can train with Angel," Mike said, his voice faltering. "I've seen a lot of gumshoes. He's one of the best I've known. Maybe one of the best there's ever been."

Barbara started to say something in response, but Slade couldn't hear it. The words were snatched away by a rushing in his ears, like a high wind. He couldn't see her anymore, either. His eyes were filled with a bright, pure whiteness, as if more layers had been added to the gauze. He thought, for just a moment, that he caught a glimpse of the cemetery, looking down on it through a cloud, but then it was gone and there was only white and wind and peace.

Peace everywhere.

Peace.

EPILOGUE

Afternoon light slanted through the windows of the
Angel Investigations office. Angel kept well back from
it, leaning on the doorjamb of his private inner office,
his arms folded over his chest. Cordelia sat behind the
desk, Doyle was on the couch, and Barbara Morris sat
in the big overstuffed brown chair.

"Barry Fetzer and a couple of Wechsler's other
thugs were picked up about an hour ago outside a
Bun Boy restaurant in Baker. They were headed for
Nevada," Barbara said. "They're on their way back
to town now."

"What's going to happen to them?" Cordelia
asked.

"They'll be charged with conspiracy in the deaths
of the guards at the San Gabriel plant," Barbara
explained. "Meanwhile the police will keep looking
for something else to charge them with."

"What about the rest of it?" Angel asked. "The cemeteries?"

When they finished dealing with the demons at the Hollywood Peaceful Rest Cemetery, they had made the rounds of a few of the other local cemeteries. Where the sprinkler systems had started, there were a few demons who had to be taken care of. But for the most part, the biggest concentration of them was in Hollywood.

Before the sun came up they headed back to the office. After the long night, Angel and Cordelia had gotten a chance to rest, but Doyle had to run one more errand, and Barbara had gone to check in at the Academy. She'd been gone for a few hours and had now returned with the news.

"There's a limit to how much weirdness the city can deal with at any one time," Barbara said. "I've heard that Harold Wechsler drowned at the San Gabriel plant. Foul play is suspected, and the police think maybe Fetzer is involved, along with the others who were picked up making a run for Nevada. There hasn't been a peep about the cemeteries, though."

"How can that be?" Cordelia asked. "Someone must have noticed that half the graves in Hollywood had been opened up and the bodies spread all over the place."

"I'm sure they were found," Barbara explained. "But someone is keeping a pretty tight lid on that information."

"Not surprising," Angel offered. "It'd be hard to explain away."

"And the press is too busy investigating why the city's water was shut down for several hours to even pick up on any rumors they might hear."

Just then the front door opened, and Detective Kate Lockley walked into the office. She wore a white shirt tucked into blue jeans, and her hair was pulled back. She did not look happy.

She ignored everyone but Angel, whom she fixed with a glare that pierced him like a searchlight through the dark of night. "You," she said sternly. "I need to talk to you."

He went into his private office, and Kate followed, closing the door behind her.

"What is it, Kate?" he asked, taking a chair behind his desk.

"What do you know about Harold Wechsler?"

He shrugged. "What you told me. Heads up the Department of Water and Power, right?"

"Used to," Kate said. "Past tense."

"What do you mean?"

"He drowned today at the main water treatment plant."

"I'm sorry to hear that," Angel said.

"I just bet you are. I suppose it's safe to assume that the crime scene technicians won't find any trace of you there?"

"Why would they? Kate, what makes you think I—"

"I couldn't even tell you, Angel. It's just that whenever something happens in town that I can't explain, you always seem to be in the middle of it. This time, that private eye, Mike Slade, was gunning for Wechsler. You were looking for Slade. You were arrested at Wechsler's house. When I put two and two together, I only know how to come up with four."

"I've never been much good at math myself."

"Fine, be that way," Kate snapped. "How about this? I'll tell you what I know. If you can fill in any of the blanks, please do."

Angel nodded.

"Harold Wechsler, it turns out, once owned the building on Argyle Avenue where Mike Slade's office was," Kate explained. "The one Slade's body was discovered in the other day. Wechsler sold it a few months ago—between the time he was appointed to his job with the DWP and the time he actually took over. He sold the building to a development company that was going to tear it down to put up a strip mall."

"Sounds like business as usual," Angel said. "Go on."

Kate sat on the edge of Angel's desk. "We learned from the construction foreman that one of Wechsler's troops, a man named Barry Fetzer, who was, incidentally, arrested today, went to the demolition site the day that Slade's body was found there. He was trying to get into the building."

"Maybe Wechsler forgot something in there."

"Like a body?"

"Maybe," Angel agreed.

"So this morning Wechsler went to the main water treatment plant at San Gabriel, where he subsequently drowned somewhere around four o'clock in the morning. And coincidentally, someone hacked the plant's security guards into little pieces after they had admitted Wechsler and his entourage. And also coincidentally it was the three engineers running the place who shut off the water to the whole city. They claim they were told to do so by a policewoman with a brown ponytail. Who did you say that young lady was sitting out there with Doyle and Cordelia?"

"I didn't say," Angel said. "Her name's Barbara Morris."

"Okay," Kate went on. "So later, according to these same three engineers, a man came back to the plant, went out on top of the dam, and then came by and told the engineers they could turn the water on again. Which they did. The man was described as having dark hair and bright blue eyes." She shot another glance out of the office, in the general direction of Doyle. "Still nothing you can contribute?"

"It's a fascinating story, though, Kate."

"The body in the building on Argyle Avenue has been definitely identified as that of Mike Slade,"

Kate continued. "We found some dental records and X-rays for a broken arm, and they all match up. A number of eyewitnesses have also positively identified Slade as the man they saw trying to get to Harold Wechsler, one way or another. The real Mike Slade died in 1961."

"Wechsler killed him," Angel informed her.

"You know that for a fact?"

"Yes."

"Can you prove it?"

"Not in court. But that's what happened."

"Wechsler's not around to stand trial anyway," Kate said. "But if I keep digging, can I pin the murder on Wechsler?"

"I don't know," Angel said. "Maybe not. It happened a long time ago, and too many people are dead. You could lean on Fetzer, see if he knows anything."

"I'll do that."

"And if it has to go down as an unsolved case, I think Slade would be okay with that."

"You do, do you?" Kate asked him.

"I think so."

"Why?"

"I think what Slade really wanted was to know he had made a difference to somebody," Angel said thoughtfully. "That he hadn't gone through life without leaving a trail behind him. He wanted to know that people remembered him and appreciated him. And people do. Sometimes that's all that really matters."

Kate turned to face him, crossed her arms. Her face was unreadable. She regarded Angel for a long moment, until he was almost uncomfortable under her stare. He looked back calmly.

"So that's how it's going to be," she said. "Okay." She looked at him for another moment. "One thing I can say about you, Angel. Since you came to Los Angeles, things have rarely been quiet."

"I didn't know you liked it quiet, Kate."

"I didn't say I did. Do you?"

He pressed his palms flat on the desktop. "Sometimes I think I don't," he replied. "And then when it's not so quiet, I wish it were."

Kate laughed at that. "I know what you mean, Angel."

Angel returned her laugh. "I wonder, Kate," he said. "I think maybe you do."

About the Author

Jeff Mariotte likes to read. Between editing comic books, writing comic books, writing *Angel: Close to the Ground* and *The Xander Years*, Vol. 2, cowriting *The Watcher's Guide*, Vol. 2, and various other novels, spending time occasionally at Mysterious Galaxy, the bookstore of which he is one of the owners, and spending time with his family and pets, he sometimes gets a chance to.

"I'm the Idea Girl, the one who can always think of something to do."

VIOLET EYES

A spellbinding new novel of the future

by Nicole Luiken

Angel Eastland knows she's different. It's not just her violet eyes that set her apart. She's smarter than her classmates and more athletically gifted. Her only real competition is Michael Vallant, who also has violet eyes—eyes that tell her they're connected, in a way she can't figure out.

Michael understands Angel. He knows her dreams, her nightmares, and her most secret fears. Together they begin to realize that nothing around them is what it seems. Someone is watching them, night and day. They have just one desperate chance to escape, one chance to find their true destiny, but their enemies are powerful—and will do anything to stop them.

Available from

POCKET PULSE

Published by Pocket Books

3074

"Wish me monsters."
—Buffy

Vampires, werewolves, witches, demons of nonspecific origin. All of them are drawn to the Hellmouth in Sunnydale, California. And all of them have met their fate at the hands—or stake—of Buffy the Vampire Slayer.

This volume catalogs and explores the mythological, literary, and cultural origins of the endless numbers of ghoulish creatures who have tried to take a piece of the Slayer in the first four years of the hit TV show.

THE MONSTER BOOK

by
Christopher Golden
Stephen R. Bissette
Thomas E. Sniegoski

AVAILABLE NOW FROM

POCKET BOOKS

3016